BY THE GREAT
HORN SPOON!

BY THE GREAT

HORN SPOON!

by SID FLEISCHMAN

Illustrated by BRETT HELQUIST

LB

LITTLE, BROWN AND COMPANY

New York   Boston

Copyright © 1963 by Sid Fleischman, Inc.
Illustrations copyright © 2013 by Brett Helquist

Little, Brown and Company

Hachette Book Group
1290 Avenue of the Americas, New York, NY 10104
Visit our website at www.lb-kids.com

Little, Brown and Company is a division of Hachette Book Group, Inc.
The Little, Brown name and logo are trademarks of Hachette Book Group, Inc.

The publisher is not responsible for websites (or their content) that are not owned by the publisher.

First Revised Paperback Edition: April 2013
First Paperback Edition: April 1988
First published in hardcover in January 1963 by Little, Brown and Company

Library of Congress Catalog Card No. 63-13459

ISBN 978-0-316-28577-3 (hc)
ISBN 978-0-316-28612-1 (pb)

45

LSC-C

Printed in the United States of America

Book design by Saho Fujii

For Betty

"By the Great Horn Spoon!"

—Favorite expression of the '49ers

CONTENTS

1 The Stowaways.....1

2 How to Catch a Thief.....17

3 News of the *Sea Raven*.....29

4 The Pig Hunt.....39

5 Land of Fire.....51

6 Spoiled Potatoes.....60

7 End of the Race.....71

8 Saved by a Whisker.....83

9 The Man in the Jipijapa Hat.....97

10 The Rogue Out-Rogued.....103

11 Jamoka Jack.....113

12 Bullwhip.....129

13 A Bushel of Neckties.....136

14 The Prospectors.....153

15 The Man Who Couldn't Sit Down.....159

16 The Gravediggers.....170

17 The Fifteenth of August.....180

18 Arrival at the Long Wharf.....192

BY THE GREAT
HORN SPOON!

① The Stowaways

A **SAILING SHIP WITH** two great sidewheels went splashing out of Boston harbor on a voyage around the Horn to San Francisco. Below decks, in the creaking darkness of her cargo hold, there sat eighteen barrels of potatoes. Inside two barrels, side by side, there squatted two stowaways.

It was not once upon a time—it was precisely the twenty-seventh day of January in the year 1849. Gold had been discovered in California some twelve months before and now, in a rush, the Gold Rush was on.

The good ship *Lady Wilma*, overcrowded and heavy in

the water with cargo, thrashed her way to the sea. Her paddlewheels churned and her smokestack stained the frozen winter sky like ink. She was bound for the gold fields with 183 passengers—not counting the stowaways. Hundreds of gold-seekers had been left at the dock clamoring for passage. The California fever was sweeping through the cities and towns and villages like a heady wind. Men were buying picks and shovels and trying to get from the east coast to the west—as soon as possible and all at once.

On the second day at sea, just after dawn, the lid rose silently off a potato barrel. Cautiously, a man raised his eyes above the rim of the barrel to look about. Slowly, he unfolded his long arms and legs. Then he stood, an elegant gentleman in a black broadcloth coat. He would be the first to admit that being folded up in a barrel, with a bowler hat balanced on his knees, was not the most comfortable way to travel. Now he brushed off the hat and placed it smartly on his head. He hooked a black umbrella on his arm, for he never traveled without it, and pulled on a pair of spotless white gloves. He felt very nearly frozen solid, but permitted himself a most contented smile. Then he gave a small tap to the barrel beside him.

"All clear, Master Jack."

"Is that you, Praiseworthy?" came a young, muffled voice from the depths of the barrel.

2

"Your obedient servant," the man replied and lifted the lid.

There rose from this barrel a school boy of twelve. He had been sucking a raw potato to slake his thirst. A patch of hair fell across his forehead in a yellow scribble. He had never been so cold, hungry or miserable in his life. On the other hand, he had never been so happy. He wouldn't have traded places with anyone. His pepper-black eyes were considerably brightened with the fever of adventure. He smelled of potatoes from head to toe. His thin nose, which was smudged, felt like an icicle, but he permitted himself a most contented smile.

"We made it, Praiseworthy," he said.

"We did indeed, Master Jack."

Jack gazed at the dark cargo shapes piled high around them and listened to the scrape of the sea along the wooden hull. He thought of home and Aunt Arabella and the friendly blaze in the big stone fireplace. There was no turning back now. They were on their way to the gold fields.

"Hungry?" asked Praiseworthy.

"I could eat, I guess," said Jack, who didn't want to give the impression that he had any complaints.

"Cold?"

"I've been colder, I guess," said Jack, although he couldn't think when.

"I suggest that we see what can be done about improving our accommodations," said Praiseworthy, tapping his bowler hat firmly in place. "Shall we go?"

"Go?" Jack replied. "Go where?" He fully expected to pass the voyage below decks with the cargo. He had read dire accounts of the treatment handed out to stowaways on ships of the sea.

"Why, to pay our respects to the captain," said Praiseworthy.

"The captain!" The words very nearly caught in his throat. "But he'll put us in chains—*or worse!*"

"Leave that to me," said Praiseworthy, with an airy lift of an eyebrow. "Come along, Master Jack."

Jack gathered courage from Praiseworthy's cool assurance. As far back as Jack could remember he had never known anything to ruffle Praiseworthy's calm. In his black bowler hat, his black coat and spotless white gloves he was easily mistaken for a professional man—a lawyer, perhaps, or a young doctor—but he was nothing of the sort. Praiseworthy was a butler.

He was a butler by breeding, by training and by choice. More than once Jack had heard his Aunt Arabella say that Praiseworthy was the finest English butler in Boston. He had been with Jack's family since before Jack could remember. It seemed to him there had always been a Praiseworthy.

The ship gave a lurch and the stowaways, gathering up their two carpetbags, picked their way through the darkened passages of the hold. Jack saw barrels of smoked fish bound for San Francisco. There were thousands of feet of lumber and enough bricks to build a hotel. He saw boxes of rifles and two brass cannons—to fight off wild Indians, he supposed. And he could make out wet bundles of grape cuttings—enough to plant a vineyard.

With his heart thumping, Jack followed Praiseworthy up a ship's ladder to the creaking deck above. He was sure the captain would put them in chains—at the very least. Now the whistling of the wind came to them and the thrashing of the great sidewheels seemed as loud as thunder. They found themselves in the crew's quarters, where daylight barely penetrated. A sailor with a gold ring dancing in his ear was filling a lamp with whale oil.

"My good fellow," said Praiseworthy, "can you direct me to the captain?"

The sailor looked up with a curious squint and the ring in his ear did a jig. "The wild bull of the seas? Aye, mates." He lifted a wet thumb as a pointer. "Up there."

Up there they went, climbing another ladder to another

deck, and now Jack was sure the captain would have them walking the plank—at the very least. Wild bull of the seas! But Praiseworthy was a match for anyone, he told himself, and tried to keep a straight and firm jaw.

They entered the main saloon, where shivering passengers were swarming like bees around two pot-bellied stoves. Everyone seemed to be talking at once, and saying the same thing.

"You been hoggin' that stove long enough!"

"I got here first!"

"Let me in, pardner!"

Jack saw men of every description and some who defied description. There were lanky farm boys in rough boots and dandies in tight pantaloons. There were Yankees in beaver hats and Southerners in planters' hats. There were tradesmen and politicians, Frenchmen and Dutchmen, fat men and thin ones, gentlemen and scoundrels—with not a woman among them. They were bound for the gold fields, which was no place for women and children.

"Gimme a turn at that stove, gents!"

"Stop pushing, sir!"

Praiseworthy tapped the nearest gold-seeker on the shoulder, a frock-coated man with a sword cane, and inquired, "Can you direct me to the captain, sir?"

The man lifted his sword cane and pointed. "Up there, up there," he snapped, and returned to the fray.

In due time, after climbing another ladder, the two stowaways found the captain in his cabin, with the door banging open and shut with the roll of the ship. He had just come in from deck and his wet oilskins lay in a heap. The wild bull of the seas, his legs apart, stood bent over a long table. He was trying to thaw the ice in his curly black whiskers over a lighted candle. "Well, don't just stand there invitin' in the weather!" he said, in a voice like the roar of a cannon. "Come in!"

The butler shut the door, only to have it fly open again. "Praiseworthy at your service, sir," he said. "And this young gentleman is Master Jack Flagg, of Boston, who seeks his fortune in the gold fields."

"Bah!" The ship's master, whose name was Joshua Swain, hardly bothered to look up. It was hard to tell whether he was a good man in a bad temper, or a bad man in a good temper. He had a plump nose and wore a long, blue coat with a row of brass buttons the size of gold pieces.

The *Lady Wilma* pitched and rolled and the candlestick slid from one end of the long table to the other. Captain Swain caught it just in time. "Blasted weather," he growled. "And me racing the *Sea Raven* around the Horn. Me, with my hold full of bricks and twice as many passengers as I ought to carry. But I'll beat the *Sea Raven*, by grabs—if I have to throw the extra passengers overboard!"

The door banged shut and Jack, now wide-eyed, stared at the ship's master as if he were a stout devil in brass buttons and frozen whiskers. He would give them the plank, for sure.

Again the ship lurched, the candlestick flew—but this time Praiseworthy caught it in midair. "Allow me, sir," he said, and held the candle firmly under the captain's stiff whiskers. But the wild bull of the seas wouldn't stand still and Praiseworthy was soon following him as he paced the cabin.

"Do you know what the *Sea Raven* carries in her cargo holds!" Captain Swain bellowed. "Miners' boots and flannel shirts and mosquito netting. Mosquito netting! She's so light in the water her keel is hardly damp!" Then he stopped to thaw his beard over the flame and the roar went out of his voice. "Ah-h-h," he sighed and in another moment a smile appeared in the weathered creases of his eyes. "That's better. Now then, gentlemen, what can I do for you?"

Jack exchanged a quick glance with Praiseworthy, who remained perfectly at ease. "We wish to report a pair of stowaways, sir," said the butler.

At that announcement the captain's smile vanished and he exploded again. "Stowaways!" he roared. "Stowaways! By grabs, I'll skin them alive! I'll put them in chains! Where are they!"

In his fury the captain almost set his whiskers aflame. Praiseworthy pinched out the candle. "Standing right here, sir."

"Here? *Where!* I'll skin them alive *and* put them in chains! Stowaways on my ship! Where are they!"

"Here, sir," repeated the butler.

And Jack, swallowing hard, decided to make the best or the worst of it. "Standing before you, sir."

It was as if for the first time Captain Swain noticed Jack at all. *"You!"* he bellowed, and his plump nose was red with anger. "Why—you're a mere jib of a boy. A lad of ten!"

"Twelve, sir," said Jack. "But I can do a man's work, sir!"

"By grabs, I'll make you walk the plank—both of you!"

"If I may make an observation," said Praiseworthy. "You are obviously too civilized for such pirate tricks."

"Bah!"

"Permit me to explain," Praiseworthy went on. "It was not our intention to defraud the shipping company. The moment there was posted notice of the *Lady Wilma's* departure for California, Master Jack and I were in line to buy a ticket. But in the push and clamor some clever cut-purse helped himself to our passage money, leaving us penniless. No doubt he bought a ticket for himself and is aboard this very ship, sir."

"A likely story," growled the captain.

"An unlikely story," Praiseworthy said, "but true. Naturally, we had no choice but to become stowaways. And if I may add—it is imperative, sir, that Master Jack reach the gold fields and make his fortune. Without delay."

"Bah! This California fever is spreading like a plague! New England will be left half empty in another six months, by grabs! Anything with a keel is calling itself a gold ship and putting to sea—scows with rotten bottoms, fishing trawlers, whaling ships! Argonauts of old, they are, chasing after the golden fleece. Every man-Jack thinks he will make his fortune. Bah!"

All this while Jack Flagg stood quietly listening, not only to the captain, but to the icy winds in the shrouds and ratlines. He stood straight and tried not to look afraid. He had made up his mind that he must reach the treasure streams of California one way or another—and this was certainly one way or another.

He refused to give in to a lurking homesickness, but he found himself thinking of his two younger sisters, Constance and Sarah, left behind in Boston with Aunt

Arabella. They had surely burst into tears to find him gone, run away, and perhaps they had not dried their eyes yet. But there was no help for it, he told himself.

Neither Jack nor his sisters remembered their own parents, who had been taken away by cholera. The children had gone to live with their Aunt Arabella in the big house on the bay, with almost more rooms than they could count. She was as young and beautiful as the house was old and grand. It had been in the Flagg family for more than a century. In times past the house had been filled with servants and guests and laughter, but the family had fallen upon hard times. Aunt Arabella had closed off half the rooms and no longer entertained. Of her staff, she kept only an upstairs maid, a downstairs maid—and Praiseworthy.

And then Jack had overheard Banker Stites tell Aunt Arabella that her inheritance was almost gone. In another year, he warned her, she would be virtually penniless. Even the house, with all its family memories, would have to be sold.

"I advise you to fire your remaining servants at once," Banker Stites had said. "You can't afford them any more."

"But I couldn't do that," Aunt Arabella smiled. "Why, they are like members of the family. Oh no, I couldn't let them go."

It was then that Jack knew he must help Aunt Arabella. But how? At the same time, stories drifting back from California excited everyone's imagination. He had heard of men picking up nuggets the size of goose eggs and stubbing their toes on lumps the size of pumpkins. A boy could do that—even a boy not yet thirteen. Without a second thought Jack made plans to run away to the gold fields.

But nothing escaped Praiseworthy, and he found Jack out. Instead of informing Aunt Arabella, for she would never consent to such a venture, Praiseworthy kept Jack's secret—and more.

"An excellent plan," he said. "A worthy plan, indeed." For he was as devoted to Aunt Arabella as Jack himself. "I'll go with you, Master Jack. There will be ship's passage to pay. I've a few banknotes put aside." And together, pooling savings, the boy and the butler set out for the world at large.

But thanks to the light-fingered thief, the world had proved to be no larger than the inside of a potato barrel.

"Blast!" said the captain, standing at a porthole.

"There's the *Sea Raven* abeam of us now. Standing there as if to thumb her nose at us!"

Jack got a glimpse of the other ship on a rising swell— a two-masted sidewheeler exactly like the *Lady Wilma*.

"If I may observe," Praiseworthy remarked with his

perfect calm. "It is a fifteen-thousand-mile voyage around Cape Horn to San Francisco, I believe. It is not the beginning of a race that counts, sir, but the end."

"If I win the race I'll get command of a new clipper ship building in the yards. She'll be the pride of the seas, and I want her, sir!" Captain Swain unhooked the brass voice tube and bellowed to the engine room below. "More steam, sir! It's all we can do to keep up. More steam!" And then he turned to the stowaways. "You'll work off your passage on this ship, by grabs! You there, boy!"

Jack, who was already standing straight, stood even straighter. "Yes, sir?"

"You'll work as ship's boy. I'll run your legs off—and that's letting you off easy. And you, sir—"

"Praiseworthy, at your service."

"What in tarnation *are* you in that getup?"

"I am a butler, sir."

"A butler!" the captain roared. "A butler! What in the name of Old Scratch can a *butler* do?"

"It's the other way around, sir," said Praiseworthy, who took pride in his calling. "There's nothing a butler *cannot* do. I open doors. I close doors. I announce that dinner is served. I supervise the staff and captain the household—much as you do this ship, sir. A most exacting job, if I may say so."

"Bah!"

And Jack ventured, "Aunt Arabella says he's the best there is. She says there's no problem too big for Praiseworthy."

"Silence, boy! A butler, are you! By grabs, I know where there's a door you can open. The furnace door—and you can shovel in fuel! To the coal bunkers with you, butler! Now out of my sight before I change my mind and put you both in chains!"

"Sir," said Jack, trembling inwardly. "I don't care to be ship's boy."

"What!"

"If Praiseworthy is going to the coal bunkers—I'll shovel coal too." Jack met Praiseworthy's glance, but only for a moment. "We're partners, sir. Either send me to the coal bunkers or—," he gulped, "or put me in chains."

The wild bull of the seas was struck absolutely speechless.

"Don't pay any attention to Master Jack," said Praiseworthy quickly. "The boy is light-headed from sheer hunger. He hasn't eaten since yesterday and he doesn't know what he's saying."

"Yes, I do," said Jack. "You told me yourself we'd stick together—through thick and thin."

By this time the captain had recovered his voice and a smile lurked in his eye. "By grabs," he said. "By grabs, here's a lad with stuffings. He doesn't want an easy berth. Wants a man's job. All right, to the coal bunkers, *both* of you."

"Thank you, sir," said Jack, picking up his carpetbag.

The captain cocked a shaggy eyebrow. "It wouldn't hurt none if you stopped off first at the galley and told the cook I said to give you something to eat. A man can't shovel coal on an empty stomach—or a lad either. Now, be out of my sight!"

The door flew open and the stowaways withdrew. They descended one ladder and then another, got their breakfast and reported to the engineer. He pointed out the boiler furnace, the coal bins and the shovels. Praiseworthy removed his bowler hat, his white gloves and the umbrella from the crook of his arm. They made a neat pile of their coats and rolled up their sleeves.

"Unless I miss my guess," said Praiseworthy, "the wild bull of the seas is a gentleman at heart."

"I hope he wins the race," said Jack.

The stowaways set to work shoveling coal into the yellow flames of the furnace—flames that made the steam that turned the great sidewheels. Jack was eager to work beside Praiseworthy, as if it brought them even closer together. Sometimes he wished Praiseworthy were anything but a butler. It imposed a slight distance between them that

Praiseworthy was careful to maintain. Jack would be happy to be called Jack, just Jack, and not Master Jack. But Praiseworthy wouldn't hear of it, even though they were now partners.

"Praiseworthy," said Jack, wiping back the hair from his forehead. He had to raise his voice above the howl of the fire and the clank of machinery. "Praiseworthy, do you really believe the cut-purse is aboard the *Lady Wilma?*"

"I do indeed," said the butler, digging into the bunker of coal. "And we shall unmask the scoundrel."

"But how?"

"How? Why, I haven't the faintest idea, Master Jack. But between us, we'll think of something—by grabs."

While the captain went back on deck and froze his whiskers again, while the passengers huddled around the two pot-bellied stoves, Praiseworthy whistled and Jack hummed. They alone of the gold-seekers aboard the *Lady Wilma* had a roaring fire to warm them as the sidewheeler went splashing through the sleet and the wind and the sea.

② How to Catch a Thief

AFTER MANY DAYS, like a dog after a rain, the *Lady Wilma* shook winter from her masts and riggings. She entered the southern latitudes. The sun came out bright and fresh as if newly forged, and the nights were speckled over with stars. The fires went out in the pot-bellied stoves and the passengers began to shed their greatcoats and heavy woolens. In another week they were down to their shirtsleeves.

In the lower regions of the ship Praiseworthy and Jack were still at their shovels. They were powdered over with coal dust, but Jack did not mind the work. It would toughen him for digging in the gold fields, he thought. Still, the roaring flames had lost their friendliness. The boiler room was becoming distinctly overheated.

"Master Jack," said Praiseworthy, thinking of the tropic zones that lay ahead, "another week at our post and we shall be roasted alive."

But the heat did not bother Jack—for every turn of the paddlewheels brought the far country a bit closer. Even though the sea route was the long way around, it was faster than the overland trail across the plains. The ox-drawn wagon trains were sometimes a year in reaching California— and Jack was in a hurry.

Every day counted. It was fine with him that Captain Swain was making a race around the Horn. The captain was in a hurry too. Still, it would be months before the *Lady Wilma* dropped anchor in San Francisco bay. There would hardly be time enough to complete the voyage, reach the mines, make a fortune and return to Boston— before Aunt Arabella had to sell everything. But try they must.

"This infernal firebox," Praiseworthy said, wiping the sweat from his face. "We must think of a plan. We must expose the rogue who light-fingered our passage money."

The truth of the matter was that neither Jack nor the butler had the slightest idea how to go about catching a thief. But Praiseworthy was undaunted. They would surely think of something.

Meanwhile, they fed the flames, strengthened their backs, toughened their hands and slept on deck under a balmy sky. In their free time they washed in buckets of sea water and Jack began a letter home. He had no idea when or where he would mail it, but Praiseworthy had packed pen and paper and had no intention of allowing Jack to forget his duties. "But I would avoid any direct mention of our temporary misfortune," said the butler with a wink. "No point in worrying your Aunt Arabella even for a moment."

Finding a shady spot under a lifeboat, Jack spread out his writing materials and began.

DEAR AUNT ARABELLA
DEAR CONSTANCE
DEAR SARAH,

By this time you have found my note on the tea service and learned that Praiseworthy and I have joined the gold rush to California. I am writing this at sea. Please do not worry, as we are well and happy and getting plenty of good exercise.

Our ship is the Lady Wilma *and we are racing the* Sea Raven *to San Francisco. But at the moment we don't know whether we are ahead or behind, as our ships became separated in the bad weather.*

But now the sky is as blue as it can get. It is hard to remember that you are still having winter back in Boston. I go barefoot. Praiseworthy says we will soon be seeing the Southern Cross in the sky.

I am getting used to the food. We have salt beef and sea biscuits, which are very filling. For dessert we have dandyfunk, which is molasses pudding. Or plum duff, which is just about what it sounds like. You would be very proud of me, Aunt Arabella, as I eat everything.

Praiseworthy wants to be sure to be remembered. We are partners. We intend to come sailing back to Boston in a year. We will be rich as can be.

The ship is very crowded. Everyone is anxious to get to California before the gold is gone. We see other ships on the sea almost every day. They are all California-bound. I think it is going to be very crowded in the gold fields.

I will tell you about some of our passengers. There is a horse doctor with a wooden leg. There is a judge with a scar over his eye. He rolls his own cigars and carries a sword cane. They say the mark over his eye is a dueling scar. We have several soldiers who fought in Mexico. They call themselves Mexico-fighters and spend most of their time telling stories about the war. They are high spirited and always laughing.

I meant to mention that we have live animals aboard! They will provide fresh meat during the voyage. We have crates of chickens, a sow and three pigs, two sheep and one head of beef. I have made friends with the smallest pig and named him Good Luck for good luck. Praiseworthy says pigs are very smart.

It seems strange not to be in school, but I am learning things every day.

I will leave this letter unfinished and take up my pen again as adventures befall us.

The following day, toward dusk, Jack was washing up in a bucket of sea water when Praiseworthy was struck as if by lightning. "Master Jack!" he exclaimed. "You have it!"

"Have what?" answered Jack, looking up. He had had Good Luck with him in the boiler room and now even the pig was covered with coal dust.

"Why—the answer!"

"The answer? The answer to what?"

Praiseworthy's eyebrows shot up with delight. "We'll catch the thieving scoundrel at last! You've hit it, Master Jack. You have indeed."

Jack couldn't think what he'd hit, but the next thing he

knew he was following Praiseworthy like a squirrel up one ladder and then another to the pilothouse. Captain Swain turned and gave the two intruders a weather-beaten squint. His temper, if not the growl of his voice, had improved with the weather. "How is the blasted voyage agreeing with you, my hearties?"

"No complaints, sir," said Praiseworthy.

"What brings you above decks?"

And Praiseworthy answered, "You may recall that Master Jack and I suffered a slight misfortune at the very outset of this voyage. Some blasted—er, that is to say— some despicable thief made off with our funds. Master Jack here has hit upon a scheme to expose the rascal."

"Me?" said Jack.

"Bah!" the captain erupted. "I don't believe there's any such scamp aboard my ship. I asked the first mate to make a close examination of our passenger list. Gentlemen they are, most of them, and the others are too crude for the clever art of the cut-purse."

"Nevertheless," said Praiseworthy, "I believe he's among your passengers like a fox among sheep. Allow us to prove it."

Captain Swain scratched through his dark whiskers. "How do you figure on exposing him?"

"We won't expose him, sir. He'll expose himself. If

you will have all the passengers assembled in the main saloon after dark we'll know very soon whether or not you have a clever thief aboard."

"By grabs," said the captain thoughtfully. "It's worth a try."

When the sea turned black the whale-oil lamps were lit in the main saloon and the passengers began to gather. They joked and joshed, glad for something to do, for they were not used to the idleness of life at sea. Jack waited on deck with the black sow from the animal pens. He saw the horse doctor enter on his peg leg, followed by the judge smoking one of his homemade cigars. The ex-soldiers were singing:

I'm going to California
With my washbowl on my knee.

When all the passengers were assembled the captain made a grand entrance, puffing on a twisted black cigar, and with his long coat flapping almost to his knees.

"Gentlemen," he said. "I'll get to the point. I am told there may be a thief among us. A cut-purse. We can't have that now, can we?"

"No!" roared out the gold-seekers, giving their purses and money belts a reassuring touch.

"We'll string him up!" yelled a big fellow known as Mountain Jim. He had full red eyebrows and wore a bobcat cap.

The captain held up a hand to stop the voices. "This cut-purse has already struck, gentlemen. He lifted the savings of Mr. Praiseworthy and his young partner. You've seen them working off their passage at the coal bunkers. The thief may strike again. Any one of you may be his next victim. He may be standing at your elbow. I'll now turn the meeting over to the aforementioned persons, who have a plan to capture the scoundrel."

Praiseworthy, tall and calm, stepped forward. "Thank you, Captain Swain," he said. "Our plan is very simple, gentlemen. Master Jack, the sow, if you please."

At that signal, Jack led the big black hog to the center of the saloon and tied her to a post. The men began to exchange baffled glances. What had a large sow to do with catching a thief? But if there was a thief among them they wanted him caught. Their own purses weren't safe with a light-fingered fellow aboard.

"A pig is a smart animal," Praiseworthy explained.

"None smarter," yelled out Mountain Jim.

"Take this old sow," Praiseworthy went on. "She's very wise. We've discovered that she can tell a dishonest man by the mere feel of him. She squeals. Gentlemen, you can't even tell a simple lie in her presence. She'll squeal every time. A most remarkable hog, I must say."

Jack looked about at the many faces shining under the flickering whale-oil lamps. There were the horse doctor and the Mexico-fighters and the judge with his sword cane. Not even Mountain Jim, with his fur cap, was above suspicion. Jack fed the black sow a limp carrot to keep her quiet, but he began to feel anxious. What if Praiseworthy was wrong and the thief wasn't aboard the *Lady Wilma* at all?

"I assure you," Praiseworthy was saying, "that if the cut-purse so much as touches this hog, she will squeal. If you will line up, gentlemen, we'll get on with it. After the lamps are blown out and the saloon is dark, come up to the sow one by one. Touch her with your right index finger. When she squeals we'll have our thief!"

"I'm for it," one of the ex-soldiers said.

"Me, too."

"A good plan," said the judge.

"Suits me," agreed the horse doctor, turning on his peg leg. "Some of you boys get the lamps. Let's see how smart this hog is. If you're an honest man, you've got nothing to fear."

A moment later the saloon was in pitch darkness and Jack held himself very still, feeding carrots to the animal so she wouldn't squeal. One by one the gold-seekers approached and ran a finger along the sow's back. A minute passed. Two. Not a sound from the hog. The passengers scuffed across the deck in their boots, touched the hog and retired. The men were silent, listening for the squeal that would trap the guilty man. Ten minutes passed, and still they came. Even Praiseworthy felt a bit tense now.

When finally the whale-oil lamps were relit, the black sow hadn't uttered a sound. She stood in the center of the saloon wondering what all the fuss was about.

Captain Swain stepped forward, scratching his beard as he looked about at his passengers, and then turned to Praiseworthy.

"Looks like you made a mistake. That cut-purse isn't aboard this ship. By grabs, I'm sorry about you and the lad there, but it looks like you'll be shoveling coal all the way around the Horn to California."

"One moment," said Praiseworthy, as unconcerned as you please. "It's true, the sow didn't squeal, but the guilty party stands in this room, sir. Gentlemen, Master Jack and I took the liberty of powdering this black sow with coal dust. If each of you will now examine your right index finger, where you touched her hide, you will find a smudge."

Every man in the saloon instantly turned up his hand—and there, indeed, was the smudge of black dust.

Praiseworthy didn't waste a moment. "But one of you, fearing that the sow's squeal would give you away—one of you approached but *didn't touch a finger to her back*. Look around you, gentlemen. If there is a man among you without coal dust on his finger—he has exposed himself as the thief!"

Almost at once there was an outcry from one corner of the saloon. "We got him!"

Passengers, suddenly angry, crowded around and Jack couldn't see who they had pounced upon.

"We'll string him up!"

"Look there! His finger's clean as a whistle!"

"It's the judge!"

"Judge, my eye! He's an imposter!"

Jack burrowed through the crowd in time to see the "judge" attempt to draw his sword cane. But the Mexico-fighters jumped in and pinned his arms back. By the time the ship's officers got hold of the frock-coated imposter, his hat was caved in and the cigar hung in shreds from his mouth. Now the crowd opened up and Jack had never seen Praiseworthy with such a fierce look in his eye.

"I suppose we'll find the balance of our money in your cabin, sir!"

"Try to find it," spat the thief, peering from Jack to Praiseworthy and back again. "Clever you are. But we'll meet again, I warn you, or my name's not Cut-Eye Higgins."

"Humbug," said Praiseworthy just as sharply.

The miners had their own ideas of justice and the suggestions went flying around the saloon.

"Pitch him overboard and let him swim to California!"

"String him up!"

"Put him in irons!"

But Captain Swain already had his mind made up. "Take him to the coal bunkers. By the time we cross the equator—by grabs, he'll think he's in Hades!"

3 News of the Sea Raven

THE BOY AND the butler moved their carpetbags into a cabin with one porthole, four bunks and six passengers. A hammock was strung up for Jack. Since Mountain Jim preferred to sleep on the floor, with his yellow bobcat cap for a pillow, there was room for all.

"Shucks," he smiled. "If I was to sleep in a bed I'd think I was sick."

Among their cabin mates was Dr. Buckbee, the horse doctor. He was going out to the mines on his wooden leg to locate a rich gold deposit. He had a map, he whispered, that marked the very spot. At the same time, he carried an alarm trumpet around his neck, day and night, in case anyone tried to take the map from him.

In addition to Mountain Jim and Dr. Buckbee there was an ex-soldier named Nath Tweedy. He still wore his forage cap and hickory shirt, and kept his rifle and bayonet propped in a corner of the cabin. Finally, there was Mr. Azariah Jones, a jolly Yankee trader who was as big as the cabin was small.

As Jack was soon to discover Mr. Azariah Jones could squeeze through the cabin door only by holding his breath.

He said he weighed three hundred pounds "barefoot and bald-headed." It amused Praiseworthy that the Yankee trader had unwittingly provided Jack and himself with their accommodations in the hold. The eighteen barrels of potatoes belonged to Mr. Azariah Jones, who planned to sell them in San Francisco.

When all of these passengers were in the cabin at one and the same time it seemed to Jack that the walls would burst. At night the chorus of snoring and snorting was a sea-going grand opera. Jack learned to fall asleep with his fingers in his ears.

When a good wind was blowing the *Lady Wilma* spread her sails and saved fuel. Day by day the sun grew more fiery. Soon there was hardly a breath of air left on shipboard. The canvas hung limp and dispirited from the yardarms. Tar oozed from between the deck planking and dripped from the rigging. But with her machinery clanking the ship went thrashing on, digging her stout bows into the equator.

Wherever Jack went Good Luck, the pig, came trotting at his heels. When Jack stretched out under the stern boat to add a few words to his letter, the porker found him and nuzzled into the shade beside him. Jack refused to scratch his back.

"I told you yesterday," he said. He must be stern. "You'd better stop following me. We've got to stop being friends, you and me, sir. I've made up my mind. If pigs were so smart they wouldn't eat so much. See how fat you're getting! Don't you know you're going to end up in the galley? Every time the cook sees you he smacks his lips. Sunday dinner, that's what you are! Go away, sir."

But the porker merely nudged Jack's elbow lovingly with his black snout.

"I told you," said Jack. "I'm not going to scratch your back any more. Let me be."

There was no reasoning with the porker. He promptly fell asleep in the shade and Jack gave a heavy sigh. There was no escape for the pig. Next week, or the week after, the cook would come looking for him with a meat cleaver.

Jack put it out of his mind and let the porker sleep. For a moment he watched the flying fish, startled by the crash of paddlewheels, leap through the air like arrows shot from the sea. Then he wrote:

I take pen in hand again, dearest aunt and dearest sisters, to tell you of our adventures to date. But first, I will say that you would hardly know me these "winter" days. I am browned to a crisp, except for my nose. It sunburns something awful and keeps peeling. Captain Swain says my nose looks like a molting chicken!

We still have had no sight of the Sea Raven, so I can't tell you how the race is coming. I certainly hope we win.

Praiseworthy wants me to be sure to remember him to you. I see I have already said that, above. He just passed by. He walks around the deck fifty times every day. He carries his umbrella for shade.

Hoping you will not worry I will confess that we had a certain misfortune at the outset of our voyage, but all is well now. I have already mentioned the "judge," who rolls his own cigars. We took him for a gentleman, but that was an error in judgment. He is a desperate scoundrel whose name is Cut-Eye Higgins. Imagine!

But he was no match for Praiseworthy. I can tell you now that Mr. Cut-Eye Higgins had stolen our money. We had to work off our passage at the coal bins. We never complained—not once.

Praiseworthy says that if it weren't for me we might never have trapped Mr. Cut-Eye Higgins, but it was really the other way around. Praiseworthy never takes credit for himself. All I did was take Good Luck to the bunkers with me, where he got covered with coal dust. That put the idea in Praiseworthy's head.

Someday, when we sail back to Boston with our pockets full of gold nuggets, I'll tell you more and make you laugh. But you will be glad to know that Mr. Cut-Eye Higgins spends his days at the fire below decks, while we have our rightful cabin.

We thought we would never find the rest of our money, which the thief had hidden. Captain Swain helped us search the cabin, lighting up one of Mr. Cut-Eye Higgins's homemade cigars. We looked everywhere and wouldn't have found the money at all if Captain Swain hadn't begun to choke on the cigar. There, rolled up inside, were our Boston banknotes!

I will mail this letter at our first port of call. Rio de Janeiro! Imagine that! Your devoted runaways are seeing the world.

*I must stop now as I just heard someone call "ship
ahoy!" Maybe it is the* Sea Raven.

When Jack looked up the captain was standing on the
paddlebox, squinting at a distant ship through his brass
long glass.

"Blast!" he scowled. "She's not the *Sea Raven*, mates.
She's a square-rigger. Becalmed, no doubt. There's not
enough breeze in these latitudes to snuff out a candle!"

It was almost two hours before the two ships came
within hailing distance. Praiseworthy finished his fifty
laps around deck and Jack locked Good Luck in his
pen. But ten minutes later the porker was at Jack's heels
again.

Captain Swain got out his silver speaking tube and
shouted across the water. With all her sails hanging like
great curtains the square-rigger seemed to Jack like some
giant of the seas.

"Ahoy!"

"Ahoy!" answered the master of the square-rigger
through *his* silver speaking tube.

"Have you seen the *Sea Raven*, sir!"

"Aye, Captain! She came steaming by a day ago."

Captain Swain lowered the speaking tube from his lips
long enough to say "Blast."

The voice from the square-rigger floated across again, "Can you give us a tow, Captain?"

"What's that?"

"I've been becalmed for a week. We're thirty-six days out of New Orleans and bound for California. Fever has broken out below decks, sir. The *Sea Raven* turned her back on us and ran. I beg you, sir. Give us a tow until we catch a wind to make port."

Jack, standing on a capstan, could tell that Captain Swain was about to order full speed ahead. But now he could be seen pacing back and forth on the paddlebox, growling and grumbling to himself. Under the tropical sun the brass buttons on his coat glowed like lumps of fire. Towing the square-rigger would slow the *Lady Wilma* to a dogged crawl. Praiseworthy too, under his black umbrella, watched the captain. Every gold-seeker aboard seemed to be holding his breath, waiting for Captain Swain to make his decision.

To come to the aid of the square-rigger could very well mean that the *Lady Wilma* might be put out of the race. She might never catch up with the *Sea Raven*.

Captain Swain rubbed his plump nose. He cocked an eye at the sailing ship with her canvas hanging dead from the yards. Then he raised the speaking tube to his lips and shouted "Glad to help, sir! We'll throw you a hawser!"

There came a wild shouting from the rails of the square-rigger where passengers and crew tossed hats in the air. Jack couldn't help being swept up in their joy and relief, and he told himself that the *Lady Wilma* might yet get back in the race. If Captain Swain didn't think of something—Praiseworthy would.

Within the hour the sidewheeler was in harness, like a sturdy ox, pulling her burden across the equator.

The great Southern Cross rose higher in the heavens. Jack's education proceeded—without books. Praiseworthy borrowed Captain Swain's brass long glass and at night the sky became their textbook. They examined strange constellations and star clouds. It was a glittering landscape never seen overhead in Boston.

"Praiseworthy," said Jack. "Was my father anything like you? I mean—"

"Nothing like me, Master Jack."

They were silent for a moment. There were times when Jack felt a great emptiness, a loneliness, that not even Aunt Arabella could dispel. Even if they should find no gold in California, he was glad to be traveling with Praiseworthy, to be sharing adventures and even misfortunes.

"Were you always a butler?" he asked.

"Always."

Jack brushed the hair out of his eyes. "I mean, if you weren't a butler, you wouldn't have to call me Master Jack as if we were at home. We're partners. You could call me Jack. Plain Jack."

"Oh, I couldn't do that. It wouldn't be proper. No, indeed."

"But I'd like it just fine."

"We mustn't forget my position, Master Jack."

"But if we strike it rich, you won't have to be a butler any more."

"Oh, I shouldn't like to be anything but a butler. Not for a moment. I was born to my calling, like my father before me and his father before him. It will please me to go on serving your Aunt Arabella. Look there, Master Jack—I believe that is the constellation of the whale. A fine sight, isn't it?"

The two gold ships, linked together like sausages, went lumbering through the sea. On the fifth day a puff of wind began to tug at the square-rigger's jibs. And then, one after the other, the topsails, the royals and the mainsails swelled out like great white clouds.

"By grabs, she's caught a wind!" roared Captain Swain, leaning out of the pilothouse window.

With a general shout, the square-rigger threw off the tow lines and the two ships parted. There was a final exchange of good wishes. Then the *Lady Wilma* kicked up her paddlewheels, relieved of her burden, and sprinted forward. She was back in the race.

4 The Pig Hunt

JACK BEGAN TO dread Sunday dinners. It was bound to be Good Luck's turn on the menu soon. The pig no longer came trotting after him, it was true, for Jack had tied up the pen to make it escape-proof. But the porker remained on his mind if not at his heels.

And then, with Rio de Janeiro only a few days away, Jack saw the cook leave the galley with a heavy meat cleaver in his hand.

Good grief! thought Jack. He's going for Good Luck!

Without a second thought, Jack went sliding down the

nearest ladder. When the cook arrived at the animal pens the porker was gone, and so was Jack.

"It's that boy," he shouted, waving the meat cleaver. "Pigs is for eatin', not for pets."

Soon, even the gold-seekers joined in the pig hunt, for the promise of fresh pork made their mouths water.

They looked above decks and below decks. They glanced up masts and down ventilators. The cook himself went searching through the cargo hold where Monsieur Gaunt, a Frenchman in the rough homespuns of a farmer, was watering his precious grape cuttings.

"Have you seen a pig down here?" growled the cook.

"No, monsieur," answered the Frenchman. "But rats— *oui!*"

The chase continued. The pig hunters looked everywhere but the captain's stateroom, which was fortunate, for Jack and Good Luck were hiding behind the open door.

"Not a sound out of you," Jack whispered. The pig, snorting out of sheer love, rubbed his ever-fattening side against Jack's leg.

"Sh-h-h-h!"

Just then the captain himself could be heard approaching along the passageway. But when he entered his cabin there was no sign of pig or boy. He hung up his blue cap, yawned and took a nap.

When he was sound asleep Jack and Good Luck crept out from under the bunk, where there was hardly room to breathe. Jack looked around, wondering what to do next. It seemed hopeless, but he wasn't going to deliver up the porker to the cook without a battle. Leaning his bristled back against Jack's leg, the pig grunted a loud word of endearment and almost woke the captain.

Jack's breath caught. Any port in a storm, he told himself, and ran. He made a bee-line toward his own cabin with Good Luck trotting along behind. At that moment Mountain Jim happened along the passageway and the pig went through his bowed legs. If many gold-seekers had joined in the hunt, others considered it sport to outwit the cook. Mountain Jim merely turned to give Jack a wink and went on his way.

Once in his cabin Jack stopped short. Dr. Buckbee was stretched out for a nap and snoring loudly. Moving on his toes, Jack approached his hammock. He would wrap Good Luck in a blanket and hide him in the hammock. But when Jack turned his breath caught again. The porker had his two front hoofs on Dr. Buckbee's bunk and had leaned his head closer to see what all the snoring was about. The horse doctor awoke. He found himself staring into a strange, grunting face. Thinking he was being set upon by map-robbers, for he was more asleep than awake, he began to blow on his tin alarm trumpet.

Jack was horrified. The trumpeting sounded like a sick elephant. It would bring the entire ship.

"It's only us, Dr. Buckbee," Jack cried, but he couldn't be heard over the blare of the horn. There was no way out of the cabin but the door, and it was too late for that. Quickly, Jack got his arms around Good Luck, climbed on a sea chest and tried to stuff the porker through the brass porthole. But Good Luck got stuck half in and half out. Jack put his shoulder to the job, but it was no use.

"You're done for now," exclaimed Jack.

Praiseworthy, hearing the alarm trumpet, was first in the cabin.

"What's this?" he said, sizing up the situation quickly. "A pig in a porthole?"

"Have you seen the cook?" asked Jack desperately. He was still pushing against the pig's fat rump.

"A few paces behind," said Praiseworthy, opening his black umbrella. "Step aside, Master Jack."

When the cook entered, together with several gold-seekers, there was no pig to be seen. Praiseworthy had taken up a position directly in front of the porthole—with his umbrella blocking the view.

By then Dr. Buckbee had stopped trumpeting. "Robbers!" he said. "Trying to get my map! I almost caught one of them. A big fellow with fat cheeks!"

"A mere dream," said Praiseworthy.

The cook raised his meat cleaver again. "There's the boy! Where's my pig?"

"Pig?" said Praiseworthy. "What pig?"

"He's got it!"

And Praiseworthy turned to Jack. "Pig? Pig? Master Jack, do turn your pockets inside out. Our chef seems to think you have a pig about you."

The gold-seekers began to laugh. "There's no robber in here—or pig either. Come on, boys."

But the cook turned at the door, squinting at Praiseworthy. "It's none of my business," he said, crossing his fat arms. "But do you even stand under that umbrella—indoors?"

"This cabin leaks shamefully," answered Praiseworthy.

"But it ain't raining."

"One can never be too careful in these latitudes," said the butler. "Good day, sir."

The cook left, shaking his head, and Praiseworthy folded the umbrella. When Jack glanced back at the porthole his eyebrows jumped an inch. The pig had vanished.

"Look!" Jack gasped. "He's—he's gone!"

"I declare," said Praiseworthy, in genuine surprise.

Jack stuck his head through the porthole and looked around. There wasn't a soul in sight, or a pig either. Jack left the cabin and ran out on deck, where he found Mountain Jim seated on an overturned barrel and playing "Oh! Susanna" on a mouth organ.

"Have you seen a black pig, sir?" asked Jack, out of breath.

"Seen him?" the mountain man grinned. "Why, boy— I'm sittin' on him." And he tapped the side of the barrel with his harmonica.

Jack wiped the sweat off his forehead and began to smile.

"Thank you, Mountain Jim, sir." The porker was safe, at least for the time being.

"I thought I'd need bear grease to get him out of that porthole. Sit down, Jack boy, and we'll do a bit of singin' to pass the time. I'll learn you how to trap a grizzly. A boy your age needs all the educatin' he can get."

Jack seated himself beside the mountain man on the top of the barrel. Soon he was singing to the windy accompaniment of the mouth organ, drowning out any snorts or grunts of protest from the pig.

Oh! Susanna
Oh! don't you cry for me,
I'm going to California
With my washbowl on my knee.

When the cook passed, Mountain Jim lifted his yellow bobcat cap with one big hand and went on playing the harmonica with the other.

After dinner and well after dark, Jack returned for the pig. A few feet away stood the small stern boat with a canvas thrown over it. He waited until the afterdeck was clear of passengers. Then he lifted the barrel, gave the porker a hug and shoved him up over the gunwale of the boat.

"Done," he said, straightening out the canvas. He supposed this cat-and-mouse game of cook-and-pig was doomed, but he wasn't giving up. "Good night, Good Luck," he whispered.

The pig replied with a snort of true love and began scratching his back on the underside of the boat seat.

Sunday passed without roast pork for dinner and the following night the *Lady Wilma* anchored off the green coast of Brazil.

*   *   *

With the coming of dawn the sidewheeler entered the channel and passed under the fortress guns of Rio de Janeiro. Praiseworthy and Jack stood on the fo'c'sle with a warm breeze snapping their trousers. It seemed to Jack that he had almost forgotten what land looked like. The mere sight of a hill or distant tree excited him. And then the sunny harbor came into view, with church bells ringing out across the water. House windows reflected the dazzling morning sun.

"Homesick, Master Jack?" asked Praiseworthy in a quiet voice.

Jack looked up. "I wish Aunt Arabella and Constance and Sarah were with us. But, of course, the gold country is no place for women and children."

"It's not too late to change your mind, Master Jack."

"Change my mind?"

The butler rubbed the tip of his sharp nose and looked down into Jack's eyes. "Cape Horn lies ahead of us. It's a bad stretch of water. Very bad, indeed, the captain tells me. The wind comes howling in like banshees and the waves can batter a ship to splinters. No one will think the less of you, Master Jack, if you leave the *Lady Wilma* here at Rio. We'll manage to get you a passage back to Boston."

Jack turned away from Praiseworthy's gaze and tightened his eyes against the breeze. He felt a welling up inside him. Didn't Praiseworthy want him along any longer? "I'm not scared," he answered, finally.

"The thought hadn't crossed my mind."

"You said we were partners."

"We are, indeed. But I could never forgive myself if—"

"Do you think we'll get smashed to splinters?"

"The *Lady Wilma's* a stout ship."

"Do you think Captain Swain's a good master?"

"None better," answered Praiseworthy.

Jack looked back up into the butler's eyes. Go home? How could he go home without his pockets full of gold nuggets? "Then I'm going on to California," the boy said. "I'm not turning back. No, sir." He wiped his nose. "But if you don't want me for a partner any more, why I'll—"

"Don't talk nonsense," interrupted Praiseworthy, with a sudden smile as bright as the morning. "You said exactly what I thought you would. But I had to be sure. You'll do, Master Jack. You'll do."

He put a hand on the boy's shoulder and Jack looked up. He could feel the reassuring grip of Praiseworthy's fingers. The butler winked. Jack smiled.

And wiped his nose again.

Above them, in the pilothouse, Captain Swain was looking for the *Sea Raven* among the ships at anchor.

Their masts were as thick as reeds in a pond. Many were gold ships, like the *Lady Wilma* herself, pausing to take on fresh water and supplies.

When the customs boat came alongside Captain Swain shouted down, "Is the *Sea Raven* in port, sir?"

"No, *Capitan*. She left us five days ago."

The ship's master greeted this news with his familiar roar. "Blast! Well, we won't tarry! By grabs, we'll sail tomorrow with the outgoing tide!"

While the *Lady Wilma* took on coal and fresh provisions, the gold-seekers invaded the city. There were Americans everywhere. Jack posted his letter. If he had found his sea legs, he had lost his land legs. The cobbled streets of Rio seemed to pitch and roll under him. Praiseworthy had to use his umbrella as a cane until the city stopped heaving about.

Throughout the day ships could be seen arriving and departing. Old friends from New Bedford or Salem or Concord met on streets thousands of miles from home.

That night, when Praiseworthy and Jack returned to their ship, their arms were loaded with exotic fruits never seen at home in Boston—bananas and pineapples and guavas. When they awoke the next morning the *Lady Wilma* was already setting a sea course with the outgoing tide. Jack stood at the cabin porthole and watched the city slip away, holding up its windows like mirrors to the pink dawn sky.

After breakfast Jack started for the stern boat with table scraps for Good Luck. Suddenly he heard the blare of Dr. Buckbee's alarm trumpet. A moment later, the horse doctor appeared from a passageway with the trumpet at his lips and his cheeks swelled out like apples. The noise brought passengers from every direction.

"It's stolen!" Dr. Buckbee wailed, pausing for breath. "Gone!"

"What's this?" said Praiseworthy, interrupting a stroll around deck. "What's gone?"

"My gold map! I'm ruined!" The horse doctor gave a final wail on the trumpet. "My brother, rest his bones, posted it to me as he lay dying in California. And now it's been stolen. Gone!"

"Cut-Eye Higgins!" said Mountain Jim.

But almost at once it was discovered that Cut-Eye Higgins too was gone. He had been forgotten in the haste of coaling and watering the ship.

And when Jack reached the afterdeck he found that Good Luck, too, was missing. Even the small stern boat was there no more. All that remained was the canvas shaped over two empty boxes and a keg.

"The scoundrel!" Captain Swain stormed. "He must

have lit out the night we lay off Rio, waiting to enter the channel. Rowed himself ashore."

"Turn back!" commanded Dr. Buckbee, waving his tin trumpet and going around in a circle on his peg leg.

"Impossible," answered the ship's master, unhappily.

"Then I'm ruined, sir. Ruined."

"Nonsense," said Praiseworthy. "I daresay there's more than one gold mine in California. You may be the first man among us to strike it rich."

Jack said nothing about the pig. In the darkness and hurry of his escape, Cut-Eye Higgins must not have realized he had a curly-tailed companion aboard the boat. Jack was sorry about Dr. Buckbee and his treasure map, but he was pleased with Good Luck's good luck. The thief had no doubt beached the pig with the boat. Jack watched the green coast of Brazil slip further away and even smiled to himself.

The porker was forever safe from the cook.

5 Land of Fire

THE DAYS GREW shorter. The *Lady Wilma* beat her way toward the tip of South America and summer faded quickly from the sea.

Jack, who had been going barefoot for weeks to keep cool, now put on his shoes to keep warm. The gold-seekers put away their straw hats and dug in their sea chests for woolen underwear. Off the coast of Patagonia Jack awoke to find six inches of snow on deck and a school of sperm whales off the starboard bow. Soon the passengers were bundled up in great cocoons of clothing. Thin men looked like fat ones, and fat men looked enormous.

For days Praiseworthy and Jack watched the crew tighten the riggings and check the canvas against the coming winds and crashing seas of Cape Horn. An air of impending adventure ran through the ship. Jack listened to tales of whaling ships disappearing forever from the roaring Cape; of square-riggers with their masts uprooted like trees; of brigs driven back by horrendous headwinds and of barks wandering in endless fogs.

"Nonsense," Praiseworthy would say. "Mere sea yarns."

But even more forbidding, it seemed to Jack, were stories told of sea captains tempted by a shorter route to the Pacific—through the narrow and vile-tempered Strait of Magellan. There, ships were sometimes cracked in two like nuts between the rocky jaws of the passage. More than one brave captain had turned back for the tender mercies of Cape Horn itself.

"Stuff and nonsense," Praiseworthy would say, even though he believed every word of it. "We may hit a bit of inclement weather, gentlemen, but our good captain will give the back of his hand to the Cape. He told me so himself. Why, the wild bull of the seas could navigate these waters with his eyes shut."

"Well," said Mr. Azariah Jones, "I hope he doesn't try *that*. It'll suit me fine if he keeps both eyes open—and then some." The mountainous Yankee trader wore a muffler tied around his face, as if he had a toothache, to keep his ears warm.

In the pilothouse Captain Swain studied his charts. The *Sea Raven* was obviously far in the lead, but San Francisco was yet a long way off. Captain Swain knew well enough of the storms lying in wait off the Horn—winds that could drive a ship back twenty miles for every one it gained. Nevertheless, the nearer the *Lady Wilma* crept to the furious tip of the continent, the more eager Captain Swain became. They were waters to test a master's skill.

Praiseworthy, who was not born to adventure, was surprised to find it decidedly to his liking. His face was weathering. On good days and bad he took his brisk laps around deck, and enjoyed the sting of the sea on his cheeks.

"I must admit," he said to Jack, "that I'm rather keen on having a look at the notorious Cape. You might watch for the fires."

"Fires?" said Jack, attempting to keep up with Praiseworthy's long stride.

"At Tierra del Fuego. The captain tells me the natives keep great fires going day and night. Keep themselves and their sheep from freezing. Tierra del Fuego. Land of Fire—that's what the name means."

A burst of spray rose from the bows and fell like rain. "Land of Fire," said Jack. "I'll watch for it."

*   *   *

Almost without warning the first storm came roaring off the Arctic wastes and bore down on the paddlewheeler. The sun went out like a match. Long, shrieking winds, loaded with hailstones, struck the ship like buckshot. The oak wheel spun out of the hands of the quartermaster. The *Lady Wilma* went teetering over on her side, digging her ribs deep into the seas.

Jack, who had just sat down to a bowl of chowder, saw the bowl fly off in one direction, the chowder in another and the spoon in a third.

"I do believe we've arrived off the Horn," said Praiseworthy, hanging onto his bowler hat.

Captain Swain lent a hand to the wheel, righting the ship and turning her bowsprit into the wind. In the main saloon the gold-seekers had been thrown together in a tangle of arms and legs. No sooner did they unravel themselves when another violent lurch of the ship knotted them together again.

The ship's bell rang in the wind. Howling blasts ripped off the tops of the waves. Riding the swells the *Lady Wilma* seemed to climb halfway into the sky only to drop with a crash into the troughs. Jack got wild glimpses of the sea through a porthole and if he was afraid he was too busy hanging on to give it much thought.

The sidewheeler burrowed into the storm. Sea water came rushing along the decks and slipped down the hatches like so many waterfalls. Sailors, in their stocking caps, were busy everywhere, battening the hatches and taking in every rag of canvas.

"A mere squall," said Praiseworthy, holding onto a post with the hook of his black umbrella. "Why, in these latitudes this is considered a fine spring day, I believe."

The weather lasted more than a week. For a day or two sea birds came out of the sky and rode the yardarms.

The gold-seekers emerged from their cabins bruised and sleepless and hungry. Some said it was harder to eat than sleep, and others said it was harder to sleep than eat.

But hardly had the seas calmed when another gale burst from the sky. Captain Swain no longer left the pilot-house. The nights were now sixteen hours long and the days a mere glimmer of light. The *Lady Wilma* continued westing, fighting for every foot of water. Her paddlewheels thrashed hour after hour and day after day.

Being experienced hands, Praiseworthy and Jack helped keep the fire roaring in the furnace. Despite the crash and thunder of the sea, the butler seemed unafraid and Jack found comfort in being at his side.

Whale-oil lamps flickered in the passageways day and night, and it was hard to tell one from the other. The nights were the worst. Jack's hammock swayed and the cabin walls swung. If Mr. Azariah Jones wasn't pitched out of his bunk it was Dr. Buckbee. More than once Mountain Jim awoke to find them both sprawled across him.

"I've known grizzly bears that were a mite friendlier than this billy-be-hanged Cape Horn!"

Headwinds battled the paddlewheeler to a complete standstill and Jack began to wonder if they would ever reach the Pacific. The *Lady Wilma* was thrashing with all her steam to stay in one place.

But then a calm would set in, like a great practical joke. The moment passengers began to snore in their cabins, fresh winds would swoop down and jerk the ship awake.

"There'll be nothing to do but sleep when we reach the Pacific," Praiseworthy pointed out.

The portholes were almost frozen over and only once did Jack get a glimpse of land to starboard. Dark cliffs seemed to hang like draperies from the misty sky, and then the weather closed in again and they were gone.

"Do you think there's any chance we might catch up with the *Sea Raven?*" Jack asked, hanging onto his hammock.

"We could pass within a hundred yards of each other without knowing it," Praiseworthy said.

"We can't get to San Francisco soon enough to suit me," put in Mr. Azariah Jones.

"I hope we win," said Jack.

"I don't think Captain Swain has the slightest intention of losing," said Praiseworthy.

For thirty-seven days the sidewheeler battered and rammed her way through crashing headwinds that attempted to drive her back. And then, on a Tuesday morning, the sun broke out, clear and sharp, and hung like an ornament in the northern sky. One by one the deck hatches opened and the gold-seekers came on deck as if from some dark dungeon. Their eyes blinked in the unfamiliar brightness of the day.

"We've made it!" yelled Mountain Jim, throwing down his yellow fur cap. "Boys, this here's the Pacific Ocean!"

A yell went up around the ship and Captain Swain leaned out of the pilothouse. His beard had grown an inch. He gave a hearty wave and then came out on the paddlebox with his long glass. After a moment of sweeping the seas he stopped.

"By grabs!" he roared. "There she is—the *Sea Raven*. And she's *astern* of us!"

Another yell went up and the gold-seekers rushed to the afterdeck for a look. There was the *Sea Raven*, indeed, trailing far behind. It seemed to Jack the most exciting moment of his life.

"A remarkable performance," said Praiseworthy. But he was baffled. It seemed hardly possible that the *Lady Wilma* had charged ahead against the furies of the past thirty-seven days. And yet, there stood the *Sea Raven* behind them as proof.

"I watched for the fires," said Jack. "But I never did catch sight of them, Praiseworthy."

Suddenly, the butler's eyes lit up. "Why, Master Jack, you've solved it."

"Solved what?"

"You didn't see the fires of Tierra del Fuego—because they weren't to be seen."

"But you said—"

"I mean to say, the fires were there, but *we* weren't."

At that moment Captain Swain had joined the gold-seekers on the afterdeck. Jack had never seen him with such a wide and merry grin glowing from the depths of his whiskers.

"I hope you gentlemen enjoyed your passage around the Horn," said the wild bull of the seas.

"Captain," Praiseworthy said with a gleam in his eye. "Master Jack appears to be onto your secret."

"What's that?"

"We haven't been around the Horn, sir."

Captain Swain gave Jack a twinkling glance. "Is that so, lad?"

"All I said was—" said Jack.

"What he means is that you have pulled off a most daring piece of seamanship, sir," interrupted the butler. "The reason Master Jack didn't catch sight of the great fires at land's end—why, the reason, sir, is that *you took the* Lady Wilma *through the deadly Strait of Magellan!*"

"The Strait of Magellan, you say!" The captain rubbed his plump nose. "Why, that's a regular ship's graveyard." And then he gave Jack a heavy squint. "Of course, it cuts hundreds of miles off the voyage around the Horn. *Hundreds* of miles. A ship's master can be sorely tempted."

"You mean to say, sir," said Mr. Azariah Jones, turning white, "that we've been bouncing around in that awful place?"

"I confess," chuckled the captain. "The lad here has found me out." Then he pointed to the *Sea Raven*. "Look at her! Following us, gentlemen, like a chick after a hen!"

6 Spoiled Potatoes

DAY AFTER DAY the two gold ships beat their way
north along the ragged coast of Chile. Black smoke
boiled up from their funnels and headwinds spun
it out into long streamers.

Jack sat on a keg and Praiseworthy stood over him
with a pair of scissors. The boy's hair had shot up like
broom-straw during the long passage through the Strait,
and Praiseworthy had no intention of letting it grow any
longer.

"Hold still."

"I am holding still," said Jack. "Still as I can."

Praiseworthy snipped away. "You'll be a young man before your Aunt Arabella sees you again, may she forgive me. You're getting your height like a sapling."

"Praiseworthy," said Jack. "Do you really think we'll strike it rich?"

"No doubt about it."

The wind carried away snips of yellow hair. "Maybe all the gold nuggets will be dug up before we get there."

"Nonsense. There'll be enough for all."

But in the privacy of his thoughts Praiseworthy didn't believe for a moment that they would be stubbing their toes on lumps of gold. Still, he must see to it that young Master Jack did indeed strike it rich. It would not do to return to Boston without a sack or two of treasure. Why, some of the passengers had brought along chests and boxes to be filled with nuggets and gold dust.

As Praiseworthy clipped away, passengers stood around watching and offering advice. Even a haircut broke the monotony of these endless days at sea.

"Needs a little more of a snip on the port side," said Dr. Buckbee, who had thrown away his alarm trumpet and regained his good humor.

"Naw," said Mountain Jim. "Work them shears along the starboard beam there, Praiseworthy. That's where it wants evenin' up a mite."

A shout from the lookout drew everyone's attention to the *Sea Raven* astern. "She's stopped making smoke, Captain!"

Smoke had indeed stopped billowing from her funnel. Captain Swain came out on deck and gave the ship a squint.

"Her coal bunkers are empty," he said. "She went around the Horn. We saved fuel slipping through the Strait. But we're not in much better shape ourselves gentlemen. If this wind doesn't turn around—we'll be burning our last lump of coal soon enough!"

By the end of the day the *Sea Raven* slipped entirely from view behind the horizon. Praiseworthy took no comfort from the *Lady Wilma's* lead. "It's the end of the race that counts," he said again.

The wind didn't turn around. It died away completely. The *Lady Wilma* was able to keep steam up in her boiler for almost a week. One day grew warmer than the next and soon the gold-seekers were peeling off coats and sweaters.

Jack shucked off his shoes and took to climbing the ratlines—the tarred hemp ladders stretched up to the mast tops. Wearing a stocking cap the first mate had given him, he would spend hours in the crow's nest seeing the world. There were times when he felt he could see almost to California.

The day came when the last shovelful of coal was scraped out of the bins. The boiler fire burned out. The merry thrash and throb of the sidewheels ceased and the *Lady Wilma* sat becalmed.

Day after day the gold ship languished on the sea waiting for a good wind to fill her canvas. A week passed. Two. And then fresh water in the tanks got dangerously low and Captain Swain ordered it rationed—for drinking only.

From the crow's nest Jack looked down on the gold-seekers wandering the decks like caged men. One day Praiseworthy came up the ratlines, bowler hat, umbrella and all, and they watched for whales to pass the time.

"Is Aunt Arabella an old maid?" Jack asked solemnly.

"An old maid?" replied Praiseworthy. He leaned his chin on the hook of his umbrella. "Your Aunt Arabella is a young and beautiful woman."

"Is it because of my sisters and me?"

"Is what because of your dear sisters and you?"

"I mean, if she didn't have us to bring up maybe she would have got married a long time ago."

The butler dismissed the thought. "Stuff and nonsense."

"Sarah said once it was because of us."

"Dear Miss Sarah is mistaken. I have no doubt that your Aunt Arabella is merely waiting for the right gentleman to come along. And I daresay he'll be delighted to gain two fine nieces and a stalwart young nephew."

"Constance said Aunt Arabella was in love once, but he died and she never got over it."

"Dear Miss Constance is mistaken, I'm sure," Praiseworthy replied softly. "No, let's have no more of this talk. Look there, aren't those sharks?"

Sharks they were and Mountain Jim, who was fishing, caught one. He called for the cook and Mr. Azariah Jones gasped, "You're not going to eat that thing, are you?"

"I shore am," answered Mountain Jim. "If he had the chance, he'd eat me, wouldn't he?"

Another week passed and Mr. Azariah Jones's eighteen barrels of potatoes began to spoil in the hold.

"I'm ruined," he wailed, pacing the hot decks. His heavy face hung slack under a large straw hat.

"Nonsense," said Praiseworthy, out for a stroll.

"I'm a poor man," groaned the Yankee trader. "I had every cent I own in those potatoes. I tell you I'm ruined."

"Then you must sell them," remarked the butler, who wished only to be of service.

"Sell spoiled potatoes? My good friend, it's clear that you know nothing about trade."

"Not a thing."

"Who do you think will buy them!"

"I haven't the faintest idea," said Praiseworthy. "But that's only because I haven't given the matter any thought."

It was a knotty problem, even for Praiseworthy. The next day the French immigrant, Monsieur Gaunt, could be seen pacing the decks in one direction while Mr. Azariah Jones paced it in the other.

"*Mon dieu*," declared the Frenchman. "I'm ruined. My grape cuttings are drying up and the captain will not give me a drop of fresh water to keep them alive. I'm ruined!"

"Then you must water them," said Praiseworthy.

"Water them!" exclaimed the Frenchman. "Water them, you say! With what, monsieur!"

"Why—with water," replied the butler.

The Frenchman shook his head. "I have fifty gold pieces in my money belt, but a thousand gold pieces will not buy me a drop of fresh water on this ship!"

"We must find a way," said Praiseworthy.

Fresh water and coal lay waiting a thousand miles further north at the port of Callao on the coast of Peru. But the *Lady Wilma* seemed rooted to the spot, becalmed and motionless.

All that day Praiseworthy racked his brain. Fine men, Monsieur Gaunt and Mr. Azariah Jones, the butler told himself, and something must be done to help them. But even if a stiff wind came up, the gold ship could hardly make port soon enough to save the grape cuttings. And not even in Callao, Praiseworthy supposed, could he find a buyer for eighteen barrels of spoiled potatoes.

"Indeed, Master Jack," said Praiseworthy. "I seem to be a failure in my first attempt at both trade and agriculture. I suppose we should, at the very least, reimburse Mr. Azariah Jones for the few raw potatoes we helped ourselves to as stowaways."

Suddenly Jack's eyebrows shot up. A thought bolted through him like lightning. He was unable to speak for a full three seconds.

"Praiseworthy!" he exclaimed. "That's it!"

"That's what?"

"You've got it!"

"Got what?"

At that moment Mr. Azariah Jones came pacing down the deck from one direction while Monsieur Gaunt came pacing from the other. Jack quickly explained and Praiseworthy's eyes instantly lit up.

"Gentlemen," said the butler, holding up his umbrella

to stop the Yankee trader and the Frenchman. "Master Jack here tells me I have hit upon a marvelous notion. Why, it's so simple—a boy could have thought of it."

"What's this?" asked Mr. Azariah Jones, his hands clasped hopelessly behind his back.

"Monsieur Gaunt," said Praiseworthy. "As your agricultural advisor, I suggest that you buy Mr. Azariah Jones's eighteen barrels of potatoes. They're a bit spoiled, but a good bargain."

"Potatoes!" exclaimed the Frenchman. "Don't make jokes, monsieur!"

"It's no joke, I assure you," said Praiseworthy.

"Confound it, Praiseworthy," grumbled the Yankee trader. "No one is going to pay me for spoiled potatoes."

"Nonsense," said the butler. "Spoiled the potatoes may be—but juicy they are, sir. Master Jack can attest to that. Why, they're like fat raindrops in brown skins. Monsieur Gaunt, you need only poke each of your grape cuttings into a plump potato. I daresay they will stay alive all the way to Callao."

The Frenchman and the Yankee trader stood facing each other in the sun, and broad smiles crept over their slack, gloomy faces.

"I'll buy your potatoes!" exclaimed Monsieur Gaunt.

"I'll sell my potatoes!" exclaimed Mr. Azariah Jones.

"I'm saved," said one.

"I'm saved," said the other.

And the bargain was struck on the spot. Jack remained silent, but stuck his hands in his pockets and felt proud of himself. Why, if he hadn't been a stowaway, if he hadn't slaked his thirst with the potatoes at hand—why, some future hillside would be left without a vineyard.

"Gentlemen," said Mr. Azariah Jones, beaming at Praiseworthy and Jack. "You'll need a few tools in the gold fields. When we reach Callao I'm going to buy you the best pick and shovel to be had."

"On the contrary," corrected the Frenchman. "It is *I* who will buy them the best pick and shovel in Callao. In all of Peru!"

With that, Monsieur Gaunt hurried to the hold and busied himself with a jacknife. He cut holes in the potatoes and slipped in grape cuttings like so many straws.

The next morning a wind from the south came up and the *Lady Wilma's* canvas swelled out in great white billows. A happy shout went up and the ship began to move through the sea. For days after that Mr. Azariah Jones stopped anyone who would listen to say, "Remarkable pair, Praiseworthy and the lad. Born traders, you know. Imagine finding a buyer for eighteen barrels of spoiled potatoes!"

Snapping winds drove the gold ship into ever warmer latitudes. Soon the Argonauts were down to shirtsleeves again and a growing excitement took hold of them, as if they could smell land in the air. Men began to trim their beards and wash their clothes. Callao stood ten days ahead.

In his stocking cap, Jack was taking on the aspect of a young sailor. The salt air and the wind had toughened his face. His eyes narrowed with a look of distance in them. He wandered higher and higher into the riggings, exploring the mysteries aloft—the footropes and shrouds and blocks. More than once the boatswain, a bantam with a voice like a frog's, chased him down, but it was like trying to keep a boy out of a backyard tree.

Hanging onto a yardarm, Jack was the first to notice a white speck on the horizon behind the *Lady Wilma*. The speck grew into sails, the sails into a ship, and the ship turned out to be the *Sea Raven*.

"She's gainin' on us!" shouted Mountain Jim.

By noon the *Sea Raven* was alongside, skimming lightly over the seas. The wind seemed to pick her up and carry her along like a feather.

"Blast!" roared Captain Swain. "And me half-sunk in the water with building bricks. Bricks! I've a notion to dump them overboard!"

By dusk the *Sea Raven* was gone, beyond the horizon— far ahead.

7 End of the Race

WHEN THE *LADY Wilma* entered the blue Bay of Callao, Jack counted thirty-one sailing ships at anchor. He was disappointed that nowhere to be seen was the high-riding *Sea Raven*.

"She's loaded up with coal and fresh water," snapped Captain Swain. "Loaded up and skedaddled!"

Nevertheless, smiles were the order of the day. After months at sea, the gold-seekers looked upon the sunny little town as if it were Paris or London. They couldn't wait to get ashore. Hardly had the mooring lines been thrown out, like bull whips, when men began to leap to the wharf.

"Master Jack, shall we go ashore?" said Praiseworthy.

"I'd like that fine," smiled Jack.

Jack posted another letter home to Boston. The streets thronged with sailors and gold-seekers, and in the distance the great Andes rose like painted scenery. The town wasn't a great deal larger than the ship they had just left at the fueling wharf, but it was land, dry land. Jack had almost forgotten the smell of dust in his nostrils. He breathed it in like perfume. The butler and the boy rode about on mules and the day had all the excitement of a picnic.

Late in the afternoon, Mr. Azariah Jones hailed them in the sunny plaza. "Look here," he beamed. "I bought the last pick and shovel left in town. Since the California fever started the shelves are bare, I can tell you. And a washpan thrown in for good measure. They're yours!"

"*Voilà!*" said Monsieur Gaunt, appearing out of the crowd and dropping a pick and shovel at their feet. "I have got my hands on the last ones in town. And a washpan, too, my friends!"

Then he stopped to glare at the Yankee trader, who was already glaring at him.

"Gentlemen," smiled Praiseworthy. "I think we can safely say that you have found the last *two* picks and shovels left in Callao. They're bound to bring us luck. Master Jack and I—"

His words of gratitude were interrupted by the clanging of the *Lady Wilma's* bell, calling the gold-seekers back to their ship.

"Hurry, boys!" shouted Mountain Jim. "The wild bull of the seas would be mighty glad to leave without us!"

There was a wild rush for the wharf, but when Jack turned Praiseworthy was no longer standing beside him. Jack's hair very nearly stood on end. The butler was gone.

"Praiseworthy!"

The ship's bell rang through the air, but Jack didn't know which way to run. He couldn't leave Praiseworthy behind. Hadn't he heard the ship's warning bell? What had happened to him?

"Praiseworthy!"

Jack was unable to move, as if anchored to the spot by the pick and shovel. He had to fight back a welling up of tears. The *Lady Wilma* would leave without them.

And then, from the doorway of a nearby shop, the butler appeared, tall and elegant in his bowler hat and white gloves. He carried the new pick and shovel over one shoulder, the washpan under an arm and a strange package wrapped in newspaper and string dangling freely from his hand. Jack had never been so happy to see anyone in his life.

"Hurry!" he cried desperately. "We'll get left behind!"

"Not likely," said Praiseworthy. "I had to stop off and make a small purchase for our good captain himself. Come along, Master Jack."

Jack tried not to let Praiseworthy see that he had been close to tears. He threw the pick and shovel across one shoulder, gathered up the washpan, and together the boy and the butler hurried toward the wharf.

One by one, alley cats picked up their trail. By the time they reached the ship it looked as if every stray cat in Callao was after them.

Before the gangway could be raised, at least a dozen assorted cats followed Praiseworthy aboard. In their stocking caps, the crew was too busy throwing off hawsers and preparing for sea to bother with the invasion of Peruvian cats.

Jack dropped the heavy pick and shovel with a clang to deck and looked at Praiseworthy's package. "A dead rat?" he asked.

"Hardly," replied the butler.

"Cheese?"

"Not likely."

"Fresh kidney?"

"Exactly," said Praiseworthy, raising the package out of reach of the cats. "Captain Swain is extraordinarily fond of kidney pie. I promised to teach the cook an old recipe my great-great-grandfather used to prepare for the Duke of Chisley."

But at the moment Captain Swain was in no temper for kidney pie. The ship had taken on fresh water—but not an ounce of coal.

"Blast the *Sea Raven!*" he was bellowing. "She's filled her bunkers and piled her decks with coal. Hills of it! Mountains of it! Taken every lump to be had in Callao. She's made sure there wasn't a cinder left for us!"

Once at sea the *Lady Wilma* picked up a friendly breeze. If her coal bunkers were empty she was at least lighter in the water and went skimming along her course. The Peruvian cats learned to bound out of sight every time the husky-throated boatswain came along, threatening to toss them overboard.

In an unguarded moment a snap of the wind carried off Praiseworthy's bowler hat. It went tumbling into the sea, filled with water and sank.

Praiseworthy was left speechless—and hatless. For

three or four days he was not quite himself. He missed the hat. He hardly felt like a butler without it. But Jack thought he looked just fine.

A week later, as the heat bore down on deck, Praiseworthy began tying a handkerchief around his head. Jack liked that even better.

"You look like a pirate," he smiled.

"Nonsense, Master Jack," said Praiseworthy.

Hoping for a supply of coal, Captain Swain dropped anchor in the Galápagos. But there was nothing to be had except a few cords of stove wood on those barren islands. And there was even less to see except the sharks in the bay.

The *Lady Wilma* pushed on. With the rush for gold, steamers were only just being sent around the Horn to the Pacific, and fueling stops were rare.

Weeks later, off the coast of Mexico, a sudden excitement raced along the decks of the gold ship. The *Sea Raven* had been sighted. She was lumbering through the sea, low in the water, weighted down by her extra tons of coal. They stood in enormous black piles on her weather decks.

"Billy-be-hanged!" shouted Mountain Jim. "We're going to pass her up!"

Jack stood on the ratlines and his heart raced with delight. The *Sea Raven* looked half-sunk in the sea. Her passengers could be seen at the rails, glum and silent, as the *Lady Wilma* pulled ahead.

"By grabs!" Captain Swain beamed, doing a little jig on the paddlebox. "I guess if there's anything heavier than a ton of bricks—it's a ton of coal!"

By the time the brown hills of California appeared off the port side, the *Lady Wilma* was well in the lead. Meanwhile, the Peruvian cats had Peruvian kittens.

"I'll drown 'em, every one," swore the boatswain. But he had to catch them first. They ran for cover whenever he approached, disappearing within seconds. They found every hiding place aboard ship and invented new ones. Jack tried hard to ignore them, for Good Luck had taught him a lesson, but in the end he was putting out galley scraps at night. Every morsel would be gone by morning.

Dr. Buckbee spent his days fishing, with the line tied around his peg leg. He would drowse in the sun until a tug roused him. But when his back was turned, the fish would disappear as if into thin air. The wily cats grew fatter.

As San Francisco and the end of their long voyage drew nearer, the gold-seekers began to trim their beards again. They packed and repacked their sea chests. They scrubbed their clothes. And they hummed, whistled and sang the same tune.

I'm going to California
With my washbowl on my knee.

Jack's thoughts raced ahead to the gold fields. What would it be like? Would there be grizzly bears and outlaws and wild Indians? Certainly, he told himself. It was an untamed place, wasn't it? What was the use of an untamed place if there weren't wild Indians and outlaws—and grizzly bears?

"We ought to have a gun," he told Praiseworthy.

"A gun? Why?"

"To protect ourselves."

"Stuff and nonsense," said the butler.

But Jack noticed the other gold-seekers busily cleaning sidearms and rifles and sharpening their knives. He wished he had a gun. A four-shooter, maybe, or even an old Army musket with a bayonet.

One bright morning, with San Francisco not more than a day's run, the bountiful winds died away. By afternoon clouds had gathered in the sky and headwinds bore down on the gold ship as if to drive her back in her wake.

With steam in her boilers, the *Sea Raven* came steadily on course. By dusk she had caught up to the *Lady Wilma*, passing with a wild shout of glee and a victorious blast of her whistle.

"Boys," said Mountain Jim. "It looks like we're done for."

"Not a bit," said Praiseworthy, on his way to the pilothouse. The *Lady Wilma* was already making a wide tack in the wind. She might be blown hundreds of miles off course. Even as far away as the Sandwich Islands. "The voyage isn't finished, sir. Not by a long shot."

But even to Jack, with the wind snapping his shirt, it seemed that the *Lady Wilma's* luck had run out. Captain Swain would lose command of the new clipper ship building on the ways in Boston. Jack dug his hands in his pockets and glanced up to the pilothouse. The wild bull of the seas didn't have a lump of coal to fight the headwinds.

Jack was asleep in his hammock when he was aroused by a strange sound. At first he thought it must be Mr. Azariah Jones snoring in his sleep. Or Mountain Jim. Or Dr. Buckbee. But they came awake too.

A deep throb ran through the ship—and then another. Then a splash of the sidewheels could be heard. Then another. And another. The gold-seekers bounded out of their bunks, some of them in nightcaps, and collected on deck. Sparks were flying from the funnel. Steam had been built up in the boilers!

"What's the captain burning?" said Mountain Jim, scratching his red whiskers. "Cats?"

"Hardly," said Praiseworthy, above the crash of the sidewheels. He gave Jack a wink. "Neither cats nor bricks nor spoiled potatoes. As any stowaway could tell you, gentlemen, we're carrying lumber in our cargo holds. Thousands of feet of it. Lumber enough to build a hotel. It occurred to Captain Swain to purchase what he needs with the ship's fuel account. Makes a fine shower of sparks, doesn't it!"

But the race was not yet won, and Jack could sleep no more that night. He pulled on an old pea jacket the frog-voiced boatswain had handed down to him, and stood with Praiseworthy at the rail. This would be their last night aboard ship after all! The paddlewheels twirled, faster and faster, and the bowsprit came around on course like a compass needle.

"It was you, wasn't it?" Jack grinned.

"Me, Master Jack?"

"You told the captain about the lumber."

"Oh, he knew it was there. But with all his storming about the bricks in the hold, he hadn't stopped to give the lumber a thought. I merely reminded him, you might say."

In the dark of morning the *Lady Wilma* had managed to gain on the *Sea Raven*. The gold ships thrashed bowsprit to bowsprit and the red glow of their smokestacks lit up the surrounding sea.

"More lumber!" shouted Captain Swain into his voice tube. "I want every ounce of steam the boiler'll hold—and then some!"

The *Sea Raven*, too, was making a final sprint. By noon the Golden Gate stood ahead of them. But the extra burden of her mountains of deck coal was too much for the *Sea Raven*. Beat by beat of her sidewheels, the *Lady Wilma* pulled slowly ahead. Wood sparks showered from her funnel. She entered the sparkling narrows of the Golden Gate and finally came out into San Francisco Bay. The city stretched out across the sand dunes like something that had sprung up the night before. There seemed to be more ships in the harbor than houses on the shore.

"Let go the anchor!" Captain Swain shouted from the pilothouse window. A moment later the anchor chain went rattling into the bay, and hats went flying in the air. Beaver hats and straw hats and even a cat or two.

Praiseworthy and Jack gathered up their picks and shovels, washpans and carpetbags and peered at the golden hills of San Francisco. The houses looked like packing boxes with roofs, and tents of every description were pitched along the dunes.

"Gentlemen," said Praiseworthy, tugging on his white gloves. "I believe we've won the race."

After a 15,000-mile voyage and five months at sea, the gold-seekers had arrived.

8 Saved by a Whisker

IN HIS PEA jacket and stocking cap Jack felt fourteen years old at least. Maybe fifteen. He stood in the bow of the whale boat and watched the Long Wharf come closer. They bumped against the boatstairs and Jack was the first out. His heart raced with the excitement of the moment. They had arrived, and he was ready to start digging.

"Not so fast, Master Jack," said Praiseworthy. "Don't forget your pick and shovel."

"And don't start diggin' up the streets," laughed Mountain Jim. "Folks might not appreciate it."

A hilltop telegraph had signaled the arrival of a side-wheeler and now it seemed as if all of San Francisco had turned out. The wharf was alive with men, women and children—not to mention dogs, mules and chickens. Seagulls flocked in the air like confetti.

Weighted down with their belongings, Praiseworthy and Jack started along the wharf. There were barrels and boxes piled everywhere. Peddlers and hawkers and hotel runners mixed through the crowd and shouted at the newcomers.

"Welcome, boys! Welcome to the fastest growing city in the world!"

"Flannel shirts for sale! Red flannel shirts, gents! They don't show the dirt!"

"Try the Niantic Hotel. The cleanest beds in town."

"Horn spoons! You'll need 'em at the diggin's. Carved from genuine ox horn!"

"Stay at the Parker House. None better!"

The wharf seemed a mile long and the noisiest place on earth. Jack was dazzled by what he saw—tattooed islanders and East India sailors and silent Chinese with pigtails dangling behind them like black chains. There were Mexicans moving about to the jingle of their heavy silver spurs and Chileans in long serapes. There were mule skinners and businessmen, and there were miners in jackboots and red flannel shirts, with the mud of the diggings still in their beards.

The city rang to the sound of hammers. Buildings were going up everywhere and a sand dredger was pounding the air. Men stood in the doorways of the shops ringing hand bells.

"Auction! Auction going on! Fresh eggs just arrived from Panama!"

"Step inside, gents. Cheroots and chewin' tobacco."

"Onions at auction! Fifty bushels just come in from the Sandwich Islands! Also calomel pills, castor oil and carpet tacks!"

Jack gazed about at this street of wonders. There was a smell of mutton from the chop houses and a sizzle of hot grease from the oyster shops. Suddenly Mountain Jim stopped short.

"Billy-be-hanged!" he said, lifting his nose in the air. "Smell that?"

Praiseworthy nodded. "It's strong enough to knock a man down."

"Makes your mouth water, don't it?"

"Not exactly," said Jack, trying not to breathe.

"It's bear meat! Real California home cookin'. Good luck in the diggin's, boys. I'm going to follow my nose."

Following up the scent like a bloodhound, Mountain

Jim crossed the street and turned into a restaurant. Before long Mr. Azariah Jones dropped away, unable to resist the lure of the auction shops another moment.

Praiseworthy and Jack continued along the boardwalk, which was hammered together mostly out of barrel staves, and reached the United States Hotel. Captain Swain had recommended it.

"A fine room, if you please," Praiseworthy said to the hotel clerk. "And I think a tub bath would be in order."

"Very good, sir," replied the clerk. He was a bald-headed man with thin strands of hair combed sideways, from ear to ear. "That'll be ten dollars extra—each."

"What's that?" Praiseworthy scowled. "We don't want to bathe in champagne. Water will do, sir."

"Champagne'd be almost cheaper, gents. Water's a dollar a bucket. Unless you want to wait until next November. Prices come down when it rains."

"We'll wait," said Praiseworthy with decision. In this part of the world, he thought, a man had to strike it rich just to keep his neck clean. He signed the register and Jack gazed at a bearded miner pacing back and forth across the lobby floor. He wore a floppy hat and chestnut hair tumbled out on all sides like mattress stuffing coming loose.

He kept glancing at the loud wall clock as if every advancing second might be his last. Jack couldn't take his eyes off the man. Tucked in his wide leather belt were a revolver, a horn spoon and a soft buckskin bag. Gold dust! Jack thought. He must have just got in from the mines!

"Ruination!" the miner began to mutter. "Ruination!"

Praiseworthy blotted the register. "How," he asked the clerk, "does one get to the mines?"

"Riverboat leaves every afternoon at four o'clock from the Long Wharf. Fare to Sacramento City is twenty-five dollars. From there you make your way to the diggings by stage, muleback or foot."

Jack shot a glance at Praiseworthy. Twenty-five dollars—each! Why, they didn't *have* that much money! But the butler didn't so much as raise an eyebrow. "We'll be taking the boat tomorrow," he told the clerk.

"Ruination!" said the miner.

"Come along, Master Jack," said Praiseworthy.

The walls of their room were lined with blood-red calico and there was China matting on the plank floor. The window looked out on the shipping in the bay, the masts as thick as a pine forest. There were not only gold ships, but Navy frigates and Chinese junks and the going and coming of longboats. But Jack wasn't interested in the view.

"*Fifty* dollars just to get to Sacramento City!" he said. "We'll have to walk."

"Good exercise, no doubt, but we haven't time for it." Praiseworthy gazed out at the distant hills across the bay. Sacramento City was more than a hundred miles up river, he had heard, and the diggings in the foothills beyond that. "Let me see. It took us five months to get this far and it will take us another five months to get home. If we are to keep your Aunt Arabella from being sold out—we have two months left. Two months to fill our pockets with nuggets."

Jack found himself pacing back and forth like the miner in the lobby below. "Ruination!" Jack said. "We've come all this way and now—we're no closer."

"Nonsense," said Praiseworthy. There was a pitcher half filled with water on the chest and he poured a small amount into the washpan. "We'll be on tomorrow's river-boat, I promise you. Now then, I suggest we wash up as best we can, Master Jack."

Wash! Jack thought. There wasn't time to wash! "How will we pay the fare?"

"Let me see. We have thirty-eight dollars left. That's a start, isn't it? Of course, we'll have our room and meals to pay. But if I detect one thing in the air—it's opportunity. The sooner you wash, Master Jack, the sooner we can tend to our financial dilemma. Your Aunt Arabella wouldn't allow you abroad on the streets with dirty ears and sea salt in your eyebrows. And don't forget the soap."

"Ruination," Jack muttered again. He might as well be home in Boston.

They washed and changed into fresh clothes and Praiseworthy gathered up their white linen shirts. They needed a good starching and ironing. Praiseworthy had noticed a laundry sign a few doors from the hotel. It wouldn't do, he told himself, to see Master Jack turn into a ragamuffin. No, indeed. Miss Arabella would never forgive me.

When they returned to the lobby, the shaggy miner was still there, pacing and muttering in his dusty beard. He glanced at Jack, a dark sudden glance—and then the butler and the boy went out on the street.

But as they ambled along the boardwalk Jack began to realize that the miner was following them. Or so it seemed for a moment. Praiseworthy turned into the laundry, a mere wooden framework tacked with canvas, and set the bundle of shirts on the counter.

"How soon may we have these back, sir?" asked the butler.

"Very fast service," answered the laundryman. His pigtail bobbed as he bowed.

"How fast?"

"Three months. Unless there is typhoon."

"Three months! Typhoon!" The man was mad, Praise-worthy thought. Or perhaps it was the entire city! "We fully intend to leave by the four o'clock riverboat tomorrow."

"Not possible," said the Chinese, bowing and slipping his hands into his flowing sleeves. "We send laundry to China. It come back three, four months—all wash, starch, iron. Unless there is typhoon. Take longer. No one do laundry here. Everything sky high. Cheaper send to China."

Praiseworthy picked up the bundle of shirts and gave Jack a look of modest defeat. "Since we've managed without baths, I daresay we can do without starched shirts. Come along."

They had hardly gone half a block when Jack saw the miner in the floppy hat once again behind them. The black pistol in his belt suddenly looked larger. But Jack said nothing. The miner could want nothing with them. Nothing at all.

He was still at their heels when the butler and the boy crossed the street. Now Jack was beginning to feel anxious. Even a little scared. Finally he looked up at Praiseworthy.

"He's following us."

"Who's following us?" asked the butler.

"That miner from the hotel."

"Stuff and nonsense. The streets are free to everyone."

"But he's following us, Praiseworthy."

"Nothing to fear in broad daylight, Master Jack."

They continued along the sandy plaza, still looking for opportunity, and the miner marched right behind them.

"Must be another madman," said Praiseworthy, turning. He stopped and the miner stopped and they stood face to face. "Sir," said the butler. "Are you following us?"

"Ruination. I shore am!"

"I'll thank you to go your way, sir!"

"No offense, gents," the miner said. "Been on the verge of breakin' in on your conversation, but it didn't seem courteous." It was hard to see his mouth for the fullness of his beard. "They call me Quartz Jackson, and I just come in from the diggin's. My fiancée's due in on the stage any minute. Comin' up from the capital at Monterey. We ain't never met, but we writ a lot of letters. And that's just it."

"And that's just what?" said Praiseworthy.

"We're supposed to be gettin' married. But *ruination*— when she takes one look at me, she's goin' to think I'm part grizzly bear." He whipped off his floppy hat and his dusty hair fell out on all sides. "She'll get right back on the stage for Monterey. But shucks, I ain't such a bad-lookin' gent—leastways, I wasn't when I went to the diggin's. I'm just a mite growed over, you might say.

Well, I been trampin' every street in town lookin' for a barber, but they all lit out for the mines. Don't seem to be anyone left here but the Cheap Johns."

"Cheap Johns?" said Praiseworthy.

"Auctioneers. Anyway, that's why I couldn't help starin' at the lad here."

"Me?" said Jack.

"Why, that yeller hair of yours looks fresh from the barber shop. All cut and trimmed. I figured you must have flushed out a barber and maybe you'd do Quartz Jackson the favor of leadin' me to him."

If Jack had feared the miner for a moment, he couldn't help smiling at him now. He liked the man. "No, sir," he said. "I haven't been to a barber. Unless you mean Praiseworthy."

"Praiseworthy?"

"At your service," said the butler. "It's true, I've been cutting Master Jack's hair, but only out of necessity."

The miner's face—what could be seen of it—broke into a sunny smile. "I'd be much obliged if you'd barber me up, Mr. Praiseworthy. Name your price."

"But I'm not a barber, sir. I'm a butler."

"A what?"

"I couldn't accept any money for merely—"

"Well, now, that's mighty white of you. Tell you what I'll do. I'll let you have all the hair you cut off."

Praiseworthy and Jack exchanged fresh glances. The man was some sort of lunatic after all. What earthly use did they have for the man's shorn locks? But it seemed wise to humor him, and Praiseworthy said, "I'll be glad to help you in your hour of need, sir. Consider it a modest wedding present."

Twenty minutes later the miner was seated on a nail keg in a corner of the hotel porch, and Praiseworthy was snipping away with the shears. Quartz Jackson insisted that every lock be caught as it fell. Jack was kept busy holding a washpan under Praiseworthy's busy scissors. It worried him that time was wasting and they were yet to make their boat fare. But he knew it would have been impossible for Praiseworthy to turn his back on a gentleman in distress—even a peculiar miner like Mr. Quartz Jackson.

"My, ain't the town growed, though," said the miner. "Must be all of four-five thousands folks in the place. You gents figure on goin' to the diggin's?"

"We do indeed," said Praiseworthy.

"I come from Hangtown. The boys have been locatin' a good lot of color up that way."

"Color?"

"The yeller stuff. Gold. If you get up Hangtown way, tell 'em you're a friend of Quartz Jackson. Tell 'em I'll be comin' home with my bride in a couple of weeks. Shore is nice of you to shear me this way. Would you mind trimmin' the beard while you're at it? Always itchin', and I can hardly find my mouth to spit with. Jack, young Jack, a bit of sideburn is gettin' away in the breeze. Wouldn't want you to lose any."

"Yes, sir," said Jack, catching the lock of hair.

Quartz Jackson's face began to appear, snip by snip, like a statue being chipped out of stone. When Praiseworthy had finished the miner turned to look at himself in the hotel window pane, and he almost jumped out of his jackboots.

"By the Great Horn Spoon!" he said. "Is that *me?*" Quartz Jackson was obviously pleased. "Why, I'd forgot I was so young!"

Quartz Jackson was a fine-looking gent at that, Jack thought. He had good teeth and an easy smile. Except for his revolver, his horn spoon and his red flannel shirt, he hardly seemed the same man. But what did he expect them to do with the hair cuttings? Stuff a mattress?

"Your fiancée will be very pleased," smiled Praiseworthy. "Our congratulations on your forthcoming marriage, sir."

"Much obliged, Praiseworthy. You saved me from certain ruination. The least I can do is learn you how to work a gold pan. Water boy! You there! Fetch us a bucket of dew over here."

The miner paid for the water by taking a pinch of fine gold dust from his buckskin pouch. Jack was eager to get the hang of mining and Quartz Jackson, peculiar or not, was clearly an expert.

"Gimme the washpan, Jack, young Jack."

Jack handed over the tin pan, piled high with chestnut whiskers and trimmings. The miner wet them down with fresh water and began to swish the pan around.

"Gold's heavy," he explained. "Nothin' heavier. Even the yeller dust sinks to the bottom if you keep workin' the pan. Like this."

Then he handed the washpan to Jack and taught him the motion. The water turned brown from the dirt and mud that had gathered in Quartz Jackson's whiskers and hair. Finally he poured off everything—everything but a thin residue at the bottom of the pan. Jack's eyes opened like blossoms.

Gold dust!

"Why, look there!" the miner roared with laughter. "The boy's panned himself some color. I figured I scratched enough pay dirt into my beard to assay out at about $14 an ounce. Since I give you the whiskers and all—the gold is yours!"

Jack had never known a more exciting moment in his life. The grains of dust sparkled like yellow fire—and there was even a flake or two.

Half an hour later, while Quartz Jackson was having a $10 tub bath, Praiseworthy and Jack were plucking opportunity from the air. They put up a sign that said,

FREE HAIRCUTS
MINERS ONLY

9 The Man in the Jipijapa Hat

IT WAS ABOUT a week before Praiseworthy and Jack
reached the diggings.

They had caught the four o'clock riverboat at the
end of the Long Wharf. Dr. Buckbee came to see them
off, but he was staying behind in San Francisco.

"I'm going to wait for Cut-Eye Higgins," he said. "He's
bound to turn up with my map. I'll meet every ship that
comes in until I get my hands on the scoundrel!"

That night, in their stateroom, Jack polished his horn
spoon. Praiseworthy had let him buy it on the wharf with
a pinch of gold dust. Finally Jack tucked it inside his belt

and looked at himself in the mirror. All he lacked was a red flannel shirt and a floppy hat. A beard was out of the question—at least for the time being.

He glanced at Praiseworthy. He wondered what his partner would look like with his whiskers grown out and a revolver in his belt. Praiseworthy was as tall as Quartz Jackson and as straight as an awning post. There were even sun creases forming in the corners of his eyes. Yes sir, Jack thought, Praiseworthy would make a fine-looking gent.

Their adventure in barbering had paid expenses nicely. There was gold dust left over and Praiseworthy had poured it into the little finger of his left white glove. For safe keeping. He had made a list of the gold camps the miners had bandied about and now he studied the names.

"Chili Gulch, Grizzly Flats, Timbuctoo," he muttered. "They sound like dreadful places to take a growing boy."

They sounded glorious to Jack. "Don't worry about me, Praiseworthy."

"I'm thinking of your Aunt Arabella. What would she think if you write from a place like Bedbug or Whiskey Flat or Hangtown? Angels Camp—she might approve of that. But they say it's a fearful place. Let me see. There's Rough and Ready, there's You Bet and there's Humbug.

Not to mention Rawhide, Roaring Camp and Cut Throat. Well, what'll it be Master Jack? One place sounds as blood-thirsty as the next."

"Hangtown!" said Jack.

"Then Hangtown it is," said Praiseworthy.

The following morning Jack saw Indians for the first time in his life. They came to the banks of the river to watch the crowded boat and listen to the ringing of its pilothouse bell. Jack stared back in fascination. Wouldn't his sisters Constance and Sarah be frightened! But that night, when the flat-bottomed riverboat got stuck on a sand bar, Jack felt a little uneasy himself. What if the savages came aboard when the passengers were asleep—and helped themselves to a few scalps!

"Stuff and nonsense," Praiseworthy smiled, shaving himself at the cabin mirror. "The steward tells me they're Digger Indians. Quite tame. They dig for roots and acorns and are a menace to nothing but wasps and grasshoppers—which they consider a delicacy."

With one sand bar and another, it was two days before Sacramento City came into view. A shore cannon went off, raising a cloud of dust, to announce the arrival of the boat. Townspeople flocked to the river. Praiseworthy and Jack carried their picks and shovels, gold pans and carpetbags through the crowd.

It was the end of June and the valley shimmered with heat. Wooden awnings stretched over the store fronts like eyeshades. As they walked along Jack kept gazing at the mountains, the great Sierra Nevadas. They stood dark blue and purple against the hot morning sky. That must be where the gold was, Jack thought, and fresh hope shot through him. They were almost there, weren't they?

A stage was leaving for the mines at two o'clock. To raise their fare the butler and the boy had no choice but to sell off a pick and a shovel. Mining tools were in great demand and prices were astonishing. The pick and shovel brought one hundred dollars—each.

After paying their stage fare Praiseworthy poured the gold dust left over into the tips of all five fingers of his left glove. He had difficulty getting his hand in, but he made it. His left hand felt as heavy as an anvil. The dust was their grubstake and he had no intention of losing it to some rascal along the way.

"We ought to carry a gun, Praiseworthy. A four-shooter."

"There's no time for that now, Master Jack."

They were the last passengers to board the stagecoach. They had hardly taken their seats when the driver, a bandy-legged man in old buckskins, snapped his whip. The horses bolted and they were off to the diggings.

Jack was squeezed in beside Praiseworthy and a red-faced man wearing a string tie. He was quick to introduce himself as an undertaker. "Fletcher's the name, gentlemen. Jonas T. Fletcher, of Hangtown. I don't mind telling you that business is brisk in my line of work up there in the diggings. Glad to meet you, yes sir—socially or professionally, as the case may be."

In the seat opposite sat two Frenchmen in brand new jackboots and checked shirts with the creases still in them. Between them, and opposite Jack so that their knees almost touched, sat a man in a dusty linen suit and his hat pulled down over his face. He had been sleeping that way from the moment Praiseworthy and Jack had entered the coach.

"Don't see how a man can sleep on this road," Jonas T. Fletcher laughed. "Maybe he's dead. Ain't that a fine-looking jipijapa hat he's got? Musta bought that in Panama. I come across the plains, myself. Clear from Missouri."

Jonas T. Fletcher droned on. The team of horses raised red clouds of dust and Jack watched the passing sights as best he could. They overtook ox-drawn wagons loaded with stores for the mines, and strings of pack mules.

The man in the fine straw jipijapa hat slept on. A large ruby ring glistened from his finger. With the jostling of the stage his coat fell open and Jack could see the butt of a dueling pistol tucked inside his belt.

It was almost an hour before he awoke. His hand rested on the pistol and he tipped the hat back off his face. He looked straight into Jack's eyes with the faintest of smiles, as if he hadn't been asleep at all. Jack very nearly jumped.

It was Mr. Cut-Eye Higgins.

10 The Rogue Out-Rogued

PRAISEWORTHY REMAINED REMARKABLY calm. He didn't so much as raise an eyebrow. But he did give Jack a faint poke in the ribs with his elbow, as if to say—easy, Master Jack, easy. Leave the scoundrel to me.

"Small world, ain't it?" grinned Cut-Eye Higgins. His hand remained at rest, in silent warning, on the butt of his pistol.

"I hadn't noticed until today," said Praiseworthy. "If I didn't know better I'd think you were still in Rio."

The villain's scarred eye was set at a squint. "Rio was too hot for me, you might say. So I lit out for Panama.

Crossed the Isthmus by bongo boat and muleback—a whole parade of folks is getting to the Pacific that way. And looks like I beat you to California at that."

"I daresay you had a good map to guide you."

The man in the jipijapa hat bared his yellow teeth in a laugh. "A map? A map? Why, what map is that?"

Praiseworthy narrowed his glance. "I bring you regards from the good Dr. Buckbee."

"Well, now, ain't that neighborly of you."

The stage charged across the valley flats and the Frenchmen shook handkerchiefs in front of their noses to keep the dust away. Jonas T. Fletcher kept shooting tobacco juice out the window as if the ground were on fire.

Jack's hand fell to the horn spoon in his belt. He could almost imagine it was a four-shooter. That would make Mr. Cut-Eye Higgins sit up and take notice. Why, he'd beg to hand over Dr. Buckbee's gold map. The dueling pistol in *his* belt would be no match for a four-shooter.

But Praiseworthy didn't seem in the least concerned about the lack of firearms. "Have you met Mr. Fletcher?" he said, tugging at his left glove. "He tells us he's an undertaker. A man in your line of work, sir, never knows when he'll need the services of a good undertaker."

"I didn't get the name," said the Missourian.

"Higgins," Cut-Eye grinned. "Doc Higgins. Dentist."

"Well, now," smiled the undertaker. "The boys will be glad to have a tooth extractor in camp."

Praiseworthy winked at Jack. The imposter had apparently given up his judgeship. A dentist, was he? Specializing in extracting gold teeth, no doubt.

"And now if you gentlemen will excuse me," said the butler, "I believe I'll catch a nap."

Sleep! Jack thought. How could anyone *sleep* with Mr. Cut-Eye Higgins sitting there! But before the stage had traveled another quarter of a mile, Praiseworthy was napping soundly. Jack sat gazing at the villain, their knees almost touching, and the man in the jipijapa hat gazed back at him.

By late afternoon they had reached the brown foothills and the stage pulled up at a relay station for a change of horses. With the mountains rising at their shoulders, Praiseworthy and Jack stood at the well refreshing themselves with dippers of cool water. The four-horse team was being replaced with a team of six for the hard climb ahead.

"Do you think he's got Dr. Buckbee's map with him?" Jack whispered.

"No doubt about it," said Praiseworthy. "I'll wager he doesn't take his hand off that dueling pistol even when he sleeps."

"We'll need a shotgun to get the map away from him. A four-shooter, at least."

"Lacking one and the other," said the butler, "we'll have to rely on our wits, Master Jack. I have no intention of allowing Dr. Buckbee to be cheated of his map."

Soon they were under way again. The narrow road climbed sharply. Oak trees gave way to shadow-darkened pines. The sun was setting across the valley, as if to desert them, and the driver's whip cracked in the air like rifle shots.

Inside the wooden coach the passengers sat knee to knee, as before, and held on against the bumps and ruts of the road.

Finally the stage rounded a bend and the trail seemed to shoot up like a ladder.

"Ever'body out," shouted the driver. "Push, gents, push."

Cut-Eye Higgins didn't take his hand off the pistol butt for a moment. He pushed with one hand. Slowly the stagecoach, piled high on top with luggage and supplies, climbed the road. The driver urged the team on with his whip.

"Keep at it, gents! We're gainin'!"

Jack put his shoulder to the coach, like the others, and dug his shoes in the dirt. Halfway up the hill it seemed to him the driver must have six whips in his hands for all the noise he was making.

Suddenly a window shattered and then another. And just as suddenly Jack became aware that it wasn't only the crack of the whip in the air.

Gunshots!

"Road agents!" the driver yelled. He set the brake and reached for his rifle. "Holdup!"

Praiseworthy pushed Jack under the coach. Jonas T. Fletcher had beat him there. Through the spokes of the big wheels Jack saw a dozen horsemen, with red bandanas around their faces, charge out of the pines. Cut-Eye Higgins drew his dueling pistol and fired. He missed.

He didn't have a chance to reload. The road agents had them surrounded, their guns and rifles bristling in the twilight.

The leader, a big fellow with holes in his boots, called to the driver. "Throw down your rifle. The rest of you reach for the sky—or I'll send you there pronto."

Jack swallowed hard and came out in the open. Praiseworthy gave him a reassuring glance—and didn't seem scared at all. They raised their hands. Cut-Eye Higgins growled to himself, but his arms shot up like the others.

"Sorry to interrupt your journey," said the leader. "We'll only detain you a moment. Boys, hop to it." Two of the outlaws climbed to the top of the stage and threw down the trunks and boxes and carpetbags. Others broke them open to paw through the contents for valuables.

Meanwhile, another pair of road agents made quick work of the passengers. They pulled watches and chains off vests, and tugged buckskin pouches of gold dust from pockets and belts. Jack tried not to look up at Praiseworthy's white gloves. The outlaws would never think of looking *there*, would they?

"All right, gents," said one of the gang, through the bandana across his mouth. "Now lower your hands one by one and let's have your rings."

He started with the Frenchmen and then came to Cut-Eye Higgins. He wore a gold ring set with a ruby, like a drop of blood. Stolen, no doubt, thought Jack. The rogue is being out-rogued, but it was small comfort.

"Why, I wore this ring since I was a lad," said Cut-Eye Higgins. "It won't come off."

"In that case," the outlaw laughed, "we'll just have to chop off the finger."

Cut-Eye Higgins removed the ring in an instant, and the highwaymen roared.

"I don't have a ring," said Jack.

"I can see that, boy." The road agent moved on to

Praiseworthy. "Well, look here, we got a regular gentleman—with gloves on."

"Not a gentleman," corrected Praiseworthy. "Merely a butler."

"What's that? Never did hear of a butler."

Jack's heart began to beat faster. Praiseworthy pulled off his right hand glove. Their gold dust, their grubstake would soon be exposed. But Praiseworthy seemed unconcerned as could be.

"How about the other hand?" growled the outlaw.

"Naturally," said Praiseworthy. He pulled the glove off each finger, carefully but casually, and held up his bare hand. The gold dust remained in the fingers of the glove. "No rings, as you see."

And the outlaw moved on. Praiseworthy gave Jack a wink without winking and very calmly pulled the gloves on again.

But another big fellow was emptying Praiseworthy's carpetbag in the dirt—shirts, cuff links, hair brush. "Why, look here," the ruffian chuckled. "A picture. A regular beauty, ain't she?"

Jack recognized the tintype at once. It was his Aunt Arabella! He didn't know Praiseworthy had her picture along! When he glanced up, Praiseworthy had gone white with anger.

"I'll thank you to return that picture to my bag," he warned, stamping each word out of cold steel.

"You don't say! Why, I'll be proud to own a picture like this. I guess I'll just take it along."

The rest happened so fast that Jack missed half of it in the blink of an eye. Praiseworthy, in his fury, struck like a bolt of lightning. Grabbing the ruffian to his feet by the shirt front, he slammed his left gloved fist into the man's bandana-covered face. The outlaw hurled back as if he'd been struck with a stick of cord wood. And he just lay there.

"Why look at that," said the undertaker in awe. "Knocked that big fella fifteen feet *up hill!*"

If his fellow outlaws had held their fire it was only because they were too startled by the butler's awesome left jab. They were like trees growing from the ground they stood on. And then their leader seemed to grin behind his bandana.

"I'd take my hat off to ya," he said, "but it ain't fittin' for a man in my line of work. That was something to see. Boys, lift our fallen friend across his saddle and we'll be goin'."

Jack gazed at Praiseworthy with fresh admiration. The butler had never let on that he was so handy with his fists. The truth of the matter was that Praiseworthy had been as surprised as the others to see the brute go flying. And then he remembered the heavy gold dust packed in the fingertips of the glove. It was exactly as heavy as lead. With his fingers clenched around it, his fist had had the kick of a mule!

He picked up Aunt Arabella's picture and dusted it off. It seemed curious to Jack that he had brought it along; it made him feel strangely closer to Praiseworthy than ever before.

"One more thing," said the gang leader, "all you gents take off your coats and drop 'em in a pile."

The guns came up again and that left no room for argument. Jonas T. Fletcher peeled off his frock coat. Cut-Eye Higgins dropped his dusty linen coat. Regretfully, Praiseworthy added his fine black coat to the pile. He would miss it.

"Never met an immigrant yet," said the leader, "who didn't have gold pieces sewed up in the linin' of his coat. You won't need coats in this heat, gents, so we'll just take 'em along."

An instant later the highwaymen spurred their horses and carried away their booty of watches, rings, buckskin gold pouches—and coats.

Praiseworthy, unaccustomed to mere shirtsleeves, stood in the dust like a leopard suddenly deprived of his spots.

"Wait till the boys hear about this," said the undertaker. *"Fifteen feet up hill!"*

Praiseworthy moved past him to step in front of Cut-Eye Higgins. "I'll thank you, sir, to hand over Dr. Buckbee's map."

The dispirited villain reached for his dueling pistol and Jack stopped in his tracks. Was Praiseworthy trying to get himself killed!

"Don't bother to draw your gun," said the butler. "I was careful to notice that you never reloaded it. The map, sir, the map."

The other man stared at him out of his scarred eye and then began to chuckle. But to Jack it sounded as much like a growl as a chuckle. "You're a little late," said Cut-Eye Higgins.

"Late?"

"The map was sewn up in the lining of my coat."

11 Jamoka Jack

THE STAGECOACH CLIMBED as if it were part mountain goat. It lurched, it halted, it bucked, it leaped and it clung. At times there was a sheer drop to one side of the trail. Far below, the pine trees looked to Jack like sharp green lances waiting to skewer them if they slipped. He only looked once in a while.

They were almost at the diggings, he told himself—he'd been telling himself that for days. But at last, the stagecoach arrived, bringing a cloud of summer dust all the way from Sacramento City.

"Hangtown, gents!" the driver snapped, with a final

crack of his whip. "Looks mighty quiet today. Don't see nobody standin' under a pine limb with his boots off the ground."

A dog greeted them at the end of the street and barked them all the way up to the Empire Hotel. The passengers got out. There was road dust in Jack's eyebrows, in his ears and down his neck. Now that they had arrived he had gold fever so bad that he didn't see how he could wait another five minutes to get his shovel in the ground.

Hangtown!

Everywhere he looked there were men in jackboots and colored shirts. There wasn't a woman to be seen. The miners were coming-and-going or standing-and-talking or sitting-and-whittling. Blue freight wagons were being unloaded. Blindfolded mules were being loaded. The store shacks on both sides of the street were raised on wood pilings, like short legs, and looked as if they had just walked to town.

Jack shouldered the shovel and Praiseworthy shouldered the pick. On the roof of the stage the driver was throwing down trunks and hand luggage.

"What's the best hotel in town?" asked Praiseworthy.

"The Empire," answered the driver.

"What's the worst?" squinted Cut-Eye Higgins.

"The Empire."

Praiseworthy glanced at Jack. "Unless I miss my guess there's only one hotel in town—the Empire."

It was exactly one hour and five minutes before Jack saw the diggings. First Praiseworthy registered at the hotel. They washed. Immediately Praiseworthy wrote a letter to Dr. Buckbee, advising him that Cut-Eye Higgins was in Hangtown, but that the map had fallen into the hands of a gang of highwaymen.

"Can we go now?" said Jack, fidgeting. He had polished his horn spoon so much he could see his nose in it.

"Go where?"

"The *diggings.*"

"Oh, the diggings will still be there after lunch, Master Jack."

Praiseworthy's patience was a marvel—and an exasperation. They had come more than 15,000 miles and now they had to stop to eat. Jack didn't care if they passed up eating for a week. A month, even. He wondered if he could ever grow up to be as easygoing as Praiseworthy.

But once they sat down in the hotel restaurant Jack discovered he was so hungry that he ordered bear steak. The only other item on the menu was sowbelly-and-beans, and Jack figured you had to be *starving* to order that.

"You and the boy want bread with your grub?" asked the waiter. He was a big fellow in floppy boots.

"Why not?" answered Praiseworthy.

"It's a dollar a slice."

The butler slowly arched an eyebrow.

"Two dollars with butter on it."

Praiseworthy peered at Jack, and then smiled. "Hang the cost, sir. We're celebrating our arrival. Bread and butter, if you please!"

The bear steak was greasy and stringy, but something to write home about. Jack forced it down. After they left the restaurant Praiseworthy bought a pair of buckskin pouches at the general merchandise store and emptied the gold dust out of his glove. The index finger was springing a leak. Jack liked the new leather smell of the pouch. He tucked it under his belt, next to the horn spoon, and was beginning to feel like a miner. Then, with tin washbasins under their arms and the pick and shovel across their shoulders, they set out for the diggings.

The day was hot and sweaty. When they reached running water they saw miners crouched everywhere along the banks. They were washing gold out of the dirt in everything from wooden bowls to frying pans.

"Anybody digging here?" asked Praiseworthy when they came to a bare spot.

"Shore is," came the answer. "That's Buffalo John's claim."

The butler and the boy moved on upstream. Here and there miners were shoveling dirt into long wooden troughs, set in running water, to catch the flakes of gold.

"Anybody digging here?" asked Praiseworthy.

"Yup," came the answer. "That's Jimmie-from-Town's claim."

On and on they went, looking for a place to dig. They passed miners in blue shirts and red shirts and checked shirts and some in no shirts at all. Picks assaulted the earth and shovels flew. Weathered tents were staked to the hillsides and the smell of boiling coffee drifted through the air. After they had walked a mile and a half Jack began to think they would never find a patch of ground that wasn't spoken for.

Suddenly a pistol shot cracked the mountain air. Praiseworthy's washbasin rang like a bell and leaped from his arm and went clattering away.

"You there!" a voice from behind bellowed.

Praiseworthy turned. His eyes narrowed slowly. "Are you talking to me, sir?"

"Talkin' and shootin'. What you doin' with my washpan under your arm?"

Jack stared at the man. He had a thick, tangled beard and his ears were bent over under the weight of his slouch hat.

"Needless to say, you're mistaken," Praiseworthy

answered. "Until this moment I've had the good fortune never to set eyes on you *or* your washpan, sir."

"We don't take kindly to thievery in these parts," growled the miner, stepping forward. "A man steals around here, we lop off his ears. That's miners' law."

"Do you have any laws against shooting at strangers?"

"Nope."

Jack couldn't imagine Praiseworthy with his ears lopped off. He took a grip on the handle of the shovel as the miner came closer. His heart beat a little faster and he waited for a signal from Praiseworthy.

The miner belted his pistol and picked up the washpan. He crimped an eye and looked it over.

"It's mine, all right."

"You're either near-sighted or a scoundrel," said Praiseworthy.

Jack was ready to fight, if not for their lives—at least for Praiseworthy's ears. Just then, a flash of tin in the sunlight, from a pile of wet rocks, caught Jack's eye. He dropped the shovel and went for it.

"Is this your pan?" Jack said.

The miner's bushy eyebrows shot up like birds taking wing. "It is at that, ain't it?" Then he laughed as if the joke were on him. "I'd forget my boots if I didn't have 'em on."

Praiseworthy peered at the man. Apparently, shooting at strangers by mistake didn't amount to anything in the diggings. The miner hardly gave it another thought.

"How about a cup of jamoka?"

"Jamoka?" said Praiseworthy.

"Coffee. I got a pot workin' on the fire. Where you strangers from? Pitch-pine Billy Pierce, they call me— and I'd be rightly pleased if you did the same. Shucks, looks like I wore a hole plumb through your washpan. Good shootin', though, weren't it?"

Praiseworthy put his finger through the hole. The washpan was useless. "Perfect shooting, sir."

"No hard feelin's," said Pitch-pine Billy. "I can show you more ways to wash gold than skin a cat. Let's get the coffee. Put hair on the boy's chest. He your son?"

Jack looked up at Praiseworthy. "My son?" the butler started to explain, but the miner didn't leave a long enough pause.

"Mississippi MacFinn has his two boys with him. I hear they just struck it rich over at Poverty Hill. And then there's the Peterman boy. He and his pa is tryin' their luck at Swell Head Diggin's. What's your name, boy?"

"Jack—"

"You look powerful *clean* for a young'un. It don't seem

natural, somehow. Why, your ears shine like new-minted gold pieces."

Jack felt his face redden and he glanced at Praiseworthy. I'm not going to wash for a week, he thought. Or a month. Or maybe even until we get back to Boston!

There was an air of hospitality about the miner that pleased Praiseworthy and he forgave him the hole in his gold pan. "Sir, a cup of coffee would taste fine."

Pitch-pine Billy led them to his weathered canvas tent pitched along the slope. The coffee pot was boiling merrily. He filled three tin cans—black. Black as paint, it looked to Jack. He had never tasted coffee in his life. Aunt Arabella would be furious. He looked at Praiseworthy. And Praiseworthy gave him a nod, as if to make up for having Jack wash his ears back at the hotel.

The tin cans were so hot they felt as if they had just been forged. Jack sat on a rock to let the brew cool. Although Praiseworthy's coat and bowler hat had fallen by the wayside, he clung to the black umbrella as a last badge of his calling.

"A butler, a butler," mused Pitch-pine Billy. He drank his coffee down, steam and all. "You any relative to Hemp Butler over at Muletown?"

"The name is Praiseworthy—not Butler, sir."

The miner crimped an eye. "You don't say? Well, he

calls himself Butler, ol' Hemp does. Never knowed his name was Praiseworthy. But I always figured him for the shifty type. How about Ten-spot Butler over at Poker Flat. He your folks?"

There seemed no point in trying to make himself clear and Praiseworthy let it go. "Tell me, Mr. Pierce—"

"Just call me Pitch-pine Billy."

"How do we stake a claim?"

"Easy. Find yourself a piece of real estate nobody's workin' and pound four pegs in the corners. Put tin cans on 'em so folks can see. Rags'll do. And you got yourself a legal claim. That's miners' law. As long as you work it at least one day a month, it stays yours." He laughed and stroked his beard. "Of course, the other thirty days you got to stand around shootin' off squatters and claim jumpers." He refilled his tin can. "Why, there are places along the river where the claims is only four-foot square and the boys is diggin' out a fortune, back to back."

Jack finally picked up his tin can. The steam alone was like a dragon's breath. Now he was almost sorry Praiseworthy had given him a nod. At the first taste, the coffee bit his tongue.

"Drink up, Jack. Jamoka Jack, that's what we'll call you. A man ain't really accepted around here until he's won himself a nickname."

"Best coffee I ever tasted," Jack said hoarsely.

"Plenty more in the pot. I ground in a few acorns for flavor."

Jack winced inwardly. Jamoka Jack—the name pleased him, but he wasn't sure he could win it. The coffee stung and burned and tasted poisonous. He forced down another mouthful. He was afraid the miner would take back the name if he didn't drain the can. He tried another swig— but it wouldn't go down.

Praiseworthy, catching Jack's distress out of the corner of his eye, shifted his position. The tip of his umbrella jiggled Jack's elbow and the tin can jumped. The coffee spilled.

"It's no account," said Pitch-pine Billy. He lifted the pot and refilled Jack's can. "We don't stand on table manners out here."

Jack gulped and stared at the fresh, steaming black potion of coffee. He had to begin all over again. Praiseworthy gave him a compassionate glance. He considered it his duty to look out for Jack, but now he had only made matters worse.

"Lemme show you how to wash out gold without water," Pitch-pine Billy was saying. "Take your horn spoon, boy, and scrape me some dirt from the crack in that rock.

It's places like that the spangles like to hide, if there is any."

Jack was glad to set the coffee aside to cool. He slipped the horn spoon from his belt and turned eagerly to the crack in the rocks.

"Just a handful, boy."

Jack scraped away, gathering up river sand and bits of dead pine needles. The horn spoon worked fine. It got in the cracks. He filled the miner's outstretched hand and sat on his heels to watch.

"This is a trick the Sonorians use," said Pitch-pine Billy. "They come from Sonora down Mexico way. Water must be scarcer than gold around there. We call this dry washin'."

He poured the dirt in a small stream from fist to hand, like sand in an hour glass, while at the same time blowing on it. Sand and pine needles scattered under the force of his breath. He poured again and again and each time the handful of dirt grew smaller.

"Grain for grain, gold is eight times heavier than sand. If you blow just right, the spangles fall and the lighter stuff goes flyin'."

Jack bent closer. Finally Pitch-pine Billy had nothing left to blow. He held out the rough palm of his hand and laughed. "Boy, you struck it rich already. Look there!"

Resting in his hand were two gleaming pinheads of gold. But to Jack they looked as large as jewels.

"Put 'em in your pouch, boy!" said Pitch-pine Billy. "Easy—don't knock over your coffee."

"Thank you, sir," Jack smiled, whipping out his brand new buckskin pouch. "But—they're yours."

The miner grinned. "Anything that small, I throw back in. You and your pa can squat on my claim."

"But Praiseworthy's not—"

"There's more yeller underfoot than I can dig out. I'd be obliged if you'd clear some of it away. You got any idea how to work that tin pan of yours, boy?"

"Mr. Quartz Jackson—"

"You a friend of ol' Quartz! Why didn't you say so? Stay for dinner, hear. We'll have sowbelly-and-beans! I won't take no for an answer, hear! Now let's get our boots wet and I'll learn you how to pan. Bring your coffee."

Jack exchanged a glance with Praiseworthy. Sowbelly-and-beans! "We'd be delighted to join you for dinner," Praiseworthy said, since Pitch-pine Billy had left them no choice.

They moved to the edge of the stream and Jack took a swallow of coffee. The miner pulled a few weeds and threw them in the pan. Jack got down another mouthful of coffee.

"Around runnin' water," explained Pitch-pine Billy, "gold has a way of gettin' tangled in the roots of weeds and grass." He dipped water in the pan and washed the roots clean. He added more dirt until the washbasin was better than half full. Then he began to pan, using the same circular motion Quartz Jackson had shown them.

"You get rid of the rocks and slickens, little by little."

"Slickens?" said Jack.

"Mud with the gold worked out of it. Keep the pan workin' and dippin' and workin' until the spangles reach bottom. Fish out the rocks. See how I'm lettin' the slickens spill over the edge of the pan? It takes practice, boy. At first, you'll lose more color over the side than you'll save in the bottom. But you'll get the hang of it. Ain't you drinkin' your coffee, boy? Why, look there. We struck it rich again. Lemme have your pouch."

Jack took two hard swallows of coffee. Then he pulled off his shoes, rolled up his trousers, and tried his hand with the gold pan. The mountain water was icy, but he hardly noticed it at first. He hunted grass and weeds. Five minutes later he could no longer feel his feet.

"You're standin' in melted snow off the high peaks," Pitch-pine Billy chuckled. "Wash out enough color and you can buy yourself some boots." Then he turned to Praiseworthy. "You ain't exactly dressed for prospectin' yourself. You and your boy will be needin' a tent and a mountain canary."

"A mountain canary?" Praiseworthy asked.

"Mule or burro. There goes one hee-hawin' now. Got a fine singin' voice, don't he? What's that umbrella for?"

"A matter of habit."

"Well, it ain't goin' to rain around here for some time. But seein' as how I punctured your gold pan I don't see any reason why an umbrella won't work just as well. Lemme show you."

"But—"

Pitch-pine Billy lifted it off Praiseworthy's arm and opened the umbrella wide. He stuck it in the ground. upside down.

"If you don't mind, sir," said Praiseworthy, with a flash of impatience. "I happen to treasure that—"

"Yes, sir," the miner was saying to himself. "It oughta work fine—just fine."

Then he began shoveling dirt into the open umbrella. Praiseworthy watched with a kind of quiet horror. He'd carried that black umbrella for years and now it was being ruined before his eyes. "I'll thank you, sir—"

But by then Pitch-pine Billy had lifted the dirt-filled umbrella into the water and was dunking it. He began to twirl it by the handle. He dunked and twirled and twirled and dunked. "Why, I've panned gold in a pocket handker-chief," the miner said. "The dirt dissolves and washes through and leaves the spangles behind."

Jack, meanwhile, was working the slickens out of his pan. He'd step out of the water to warm his feet and take a sip of coffee and then return. He worked two pans of dirt without finding a speck of color, but then he didn't have the hang of it. He was losing the gold with the slickens. But he stayed with it and his feet turned blue.

Finally Pitch-pine Billy was no longer plunging the umbrella, but working with a deft, gentle, washing move-ment. He fingered out the rocks and after another moment returned the umbrella to Praiseworthy.

"Best gold pan along the river," he grinned. "I might buy me one of these myself."

The mud was gone. In its place along the black fabric of the umbrella lay a bright dusting of gold and spangles.

Praiseworthy crimped an eye and smiled at the hospi-table miner. "I think I can get the hang of it, sir."

He removed his shoes, rolled up his trousers and set to work. All through the afternoon Jack could be seen pan-ning and taking a sip of cold coffee, and Praiseworthy cut an elegant figure plunging a muddy umbrella in the stream.

Finally Jack reached the bottom of the tin can and that was that. "Yes sir, first-rate coffee, Pitch-pine Billy," he said. "First-rate."

"Glad you liked it," answered the miner with a bushy-faced grin, "—Jamoka Jack."

12 Bullwhip

CAMPFIRES ALONG THE river lit their way back to town. Carrying their shoes, the two partners were stuffed full of sowbelly-and-beans and between them they were richer by a thimbleful of gold. Jack's feet ached from hours in the ice cold mountain stream, but he was too elated to care.

His face was dirty and his clothes were dirtier. Praiseworthy's white shirt was splattered with mud. His umbrella was in tatters. "First thing tomorrow," said the butler, "we'll purchase boots."

"If we had a tent like Pitch-pine Billy," Jack said, "we

wouldn't have to sleep in that ol' hotel. We could stay right on our claim."

"We don't have a claim."

"But we'll get one, won't we?"

"Absolutely."

"And a tent?"

"Why not?"

"And a mule? He said we'd need a mule or a burro to go prospecting."

"A mountain canary, for sure," said Praiseworthy.

Jack tried to keep in step with his partner's long stride.

"Pitch-pine Billy thinks you're my father."

"I heard him."

"I don't mind."

Praiseworthy pulled at his ear. "When he gets an idea fixed in his head he refuses to have it removed. I tried often enough. But he meant no offense."

"None at all," said Jack, looking up. He liked Praiseworthy. He liked him especially as they swung along together, both barefoot and one as mud-splattered as the other. Partners were the next best thing to being related, he thought. Better, maybe. A partner didn't take a hairbrush to you—even when you needed it. But there were times when he wished he had a father, hairbrush and all.

They walked along and from somewhere in the trees

and shadows they could hear the wheeze of a miner's concertina. For days, since the discovery of Aunt Arabella's picture in Praiseworthy's carpetbag, Jack had wondered about it. The moment had never seemed right to ask, but now the questions just tumbled out. "Does Aunt Arabella know you've got her picture along?"

Praiseworthy shifted the pick to his other shoulder. "Yes, yes, the picture," he said quietly. "I'd been meaning to give it to you. I've no right to it. No right at all."

"It's only a picture. You keep it." Jack shifted the shovel to *his* other shoulder. "Why doesn't Aunt Arabella have a husband?"

"What?"

"I mean, she's beautiful, isn't she?"

Praiseworthy seemed positively embarrassed. "Now see here, Master Jack—"

"*Jamoka* Jack. Constance says Aunt Arabella was in love once, but he died, and women like that never get over it. They just get to be old maids."

"Miss Constance should be spanked," Praiseworthy replied shortly. And then he changed the subject. "First thing in the morning I must see about getting my gold pan mended."

"I'll bet Aunt Arabella would marry you, if you asked."

Praiseworthy stopped as if struck, and then he began

to laugh. "Now that is nonsense, Master Jack. Stuff and nonsense. A woman like Miss Arabella marries a gentleman—not a butler. It simply isn't done. I wouldn't permit such a thing. Not for a moment. Why, your dear aunt would be laughed out of Boston. Now let's hear no more of these fancies of yours. Come along."

They resumed their stride and Jack said no more. But Praiseworthy wasn't fooling him. No, sir. Praiseworthy hadn't carried off Aunt Arabella's picture—he would never do a thing like that. No, sir. Not Praiseworthy.

Aunt Arabella had *given* him the picture, Jack thought. Yes, sir. And the more he thought about it, the more it pleased him.

Soon the coal oil lights of Hangtown could be seen through the trees. Praiseworthy stopped to put on his shoes, but Jack just carried his.

As they came along the street, the men who sat-and-whittled stopped whittling. The standing-and-talking men stopped talking. And the coming-and-going men stopped coming and going.

Jack had a sudden feeling that everyone was staring at them. What was wrong? Didn't they have their heads on straight?

And then a voice said, "There he is."

"That's him, all right."

Praiseworthy and Jack kept walking. They passed the assay office and the Cheap John auction store and the general merchandise. A cold feeling was creeping along Jack's neck. "Maybe they're looking for somebody to hang," he whispered.

"Unlikely—at this time of night," said Praiseworthy. But he was concerned. The men seemed to be smiling and in Hangtown that might be a bad sign.

When they reached the Empire Hotel the porch loungers gazed at them in a kind of awe. A mutter of voices arose.

"Knocked that outlaw seventeen feet."

"*Up* hill."

"Nineteen feet—the way it was told to me."

"Nineteen feet and *eleven* inches. They measured it."

Praiseworthy stopped in the doorway. He looked at Jack, who broke into a muddy smile as if they had been saved from the limb of a tree. And then the butler turned, peering at the whiskered faces grinning in the yellow light from the hotel.

A miner shifted the lump of chewing tobacco in his mouth and said, "Stranger, you must have a fightin' arm like the butt end of a bullwhip. Pleased to have you in our town."

"Pleased to be here," Praiseworthy said, lowering the

pick from his shoulder. "But not under false colors. Gentlemen, allow me to explain—"

"Hey, Bullwhip, where you and the young'un from?"

"Boston, sir. Gentlemen, our good friend and traveling companion, Mr. Jonas T. Fletcher, appears to have spread a grossly exaggerated account of what happened. You see—"

"Hold on. You callin' him a liar?"

"No, but—"

"Well, did you knock that road agent *up* hill or not?"

"Yes, but—"

The miners began to chuckle and chewing tobacco went squirting in all directions. They had taken an immediate fancy to Praiseworthy and one by one they picked up the nickname.

"How long you stayin', Bullwhip?"

Praiseworthy shouldered the pick. He gave up trying to explain. It seemed to him that every man in the diggings became hard of hearing when he wanted to, and he'd had enough of that for one day. If they preferred a tall tale to the facts, let them have it.

"Bullwhip, you was there. Exactly how far *was* it?"

Praiseworthy gave Jack a passing wink. As long as the citizens of Hangtown were determined to hang a reputation on him, it might as well be the best. "Gents," he said, "from where I was standing—it looked *twenty-three* feet at least."

A miner swallowed his cud of tobacco. "O be joyful," he uttered.

"Come along, Jamoka Jack," said Praiseworthy, turning into the hotel.

Jack felt a brand new smile reach across his face. "Yes, sir—Bullwhip," he said.

13 A Bushel of Neckties

SOME TIME DURING the night Cut-Eye Higgins left Hangtown for parts unknown.

In the days that followed Praiseworthy's name and reputation spread through the diggings. He was pointed out to new immigrants as someone of consequence, and Jack basked in reflected glory. The truth of the matter was that Praiseworthy himself began to enjoy his notoriety.

And like chameleons, the two partners changed their colors to those of the Sierra Nevadas. They wore red miner's shirts and jackboots and wide-brimmed hats against the summer sun.

After a week in the diggings there was little of the butler left to be seen in Praiseworthy, unless it was the straightness of his back and the quiet reserve of his glance. And then, as if to live up to his reputation, he stopped shaving. Within a few days he began to look decidedly fierce.

Jack collected four tin cans against the day when they would stake their claim. They bought a dust-stained canvas tent at the Cheap John auction and pitched it beside Pitch-pine Billy's tent. All they lacked to go prospecting was a burro and a grubstake of beans, bacon, flour and coffee.

They shoveled dirt and panned mud from morning till night. Pitch-pine Billy taught them every trick he knew, including the setting of flea traps. After dark they filled their gold pans with soapy water and placed them beside a lighted candle stuck in the dirt floor of the tent.

"The candle gets the varmints to jumpin'," Pitch-pine Billy exclaimed. "About the only thing a flea ain't learned to do is take a bath. They hop in that soap water and drown."

But candles were $1 each and some of the miners preferred the fleas. There were days when a man was lucky to wash out enough spangles to pay for his grub. While an ounce of gold brought $16 far away in San Francisco it was worth a mere $4 at the diggings. And it didn't buy much.

Onions were $1.50 a pound. Supplies had to be freighted in and prices were high. Salt pork sold for 50 cents an ounce. Gold dust seemed more plentiful than flour. Hay was weighed out at 8 cents a pound.

"Oh, I seen some mighty fancy prices," laughed Pitch-pine Billy, frying up a loaf of bread in his gold pan. "There was a fella come to the diggin's with a jar of raisins. The boys ain't seen a raisin since they left home and their mouths began to slabber. You'd think it was caviar in that jar. Them raisins fetched their weight in gold dust. Come to four thousand dollars."

Slowly, day by day, Praiseworthy and Jack added to their grubstake. They had blankets, a dozen candles and a coffee pot. One noon Jack pulled up a tuft of grass and a glint of light from the roots made him gasp. A nugget. And then his yell carried from one end of the ravine to the other.

"A *nugget!*"

Praiseworthy dropped his gold pan and Pitch-pine Billy squinted. Jimmie-from-Town, who wore a mustache twisted into sharp points, came running over and Buffalo John awoke from a sound sleep.

Soon a dozen miners had left their claims to stand around and admire Jack's catch. The lump of gold was the size of an acorn. It was trapped in the fine grass roots like a fly in a spider's web.

"Maybe it'll buy us a burro," Jack grinned.

"Well, I dunno," smiled Pitch-pine Billy. "The *tail* of a jackass, anyway."

Buffalo John pulled the bandana off his head and polished the nugget. The miners passed it around, holding it up to the sun to watch it shine, and from that moment on it became known as Jamoka Jack's Nugget.

That night Praiseworthy and Jack and Pitch-pine Billy went to town for supper. There was a letter waiting at the hotel from Dr. Buckbee. It was written in a shaky hand.

My dear friends, your letter finds me weakened by the yellow fever from Panama and I can barely hold this pen steady. Curse that Higgins fellow and the gang of highwaymen you write of! Since I cannot leave my bed, please act as my agents in the matter. If you are able to recover my map, I will make you partners in the mine—fifty-fifty. Act quickly, I beg of you, before all is lost.

Praiseworthy finished reading the letter and folded it thoughtfully. "A generous enough offer," he said to Jack.

Half interest in a gold mine! Jack's yellow eyebrows lifted. All they had to do was get on the trail of those road agents. "We'll need guns," he said quickly. A four-shooter would fit fine in his belt, alongside his horn spoon and buckskin pouch. Maybe he could trade his nugget for a pistol.

Praiseworthy scratched through the stubble growing out on his face. "What we need is a burro."

"A burro to chase outlaws?" said Jack.

Praiseworthy put the letter in his shirt pocket. He shook his head. "We've no time for such speculations. First, those vultures no doubt ripped open Cut-Eye Higgins's coat and discovered the map. Second, they may already have located the mine by now."

"*Maps,*" Pitch-pine Billy laughed. "Why, there is so many maps floatin' around the diggin's you could paper a room with 'em. Boys, let's eat."

They ordered Hangtown Fries—platters of bacon, canned oysters and eggs. Praiseworthy turned to Jack. "What do you want to drink?"

Jack glanced up at the waiter. "Coffee," he said. "Coffee, sir—with a few acorns ground up."

*   *   *

140

After dinner Praiseworthy stayed behind in the hotel lobby to reply to Dr. Buckbee's letter. Jack and Pitch-pine Billy went wandering along the street to see the sights. The auction bell began to clang. Maybe Cheap John would have pistols to sell, Jack thought. "Let's go," he said.

"Don't mind," said Pitch-pine Billy.

The auctioneer placed a keg of salt butter outside the brightly lit tent, and the miners gathered around this delicacy like flies. They unclasped their jack-knives and carved off butter shavings and ate them off their blades.

Between the ringing of the bell and the free butter a crowd had formed and the sale began. Frenchmen rubbed shoulders with Sonorians and Chileans with Germans and Missourians with Yankees and Englishmen with Kanakas from the Sandwich Islands. There were sailors who had deserted their ships to run off to the mines, and soldiers who had left their garrisons at Monterey and San Francisco.

The auctioneer mounted a barrel at the rear of the tent. He was a paunchy man in an open vest and a plug hat.

"What'll you take for the hat, Cheap John?" someone yelled.

"Ain't for sale," said the auctioneer. "But I got ten pounds of Chinese sugar that is. What am I bid, gents? Who'll give me a dollar a pound? Dollar, dollar, dollar,

dollar—I got a dollar. Who'll give me a dollar and a half, half, half, half—two dollars. Am I bid two dollars, boys, two, two—"

"*Dos pesos!*" said a Spaniard with silver buttons down his trouser legs.

Jack waited through the sale of sugar, a wheelbarrow, tin pans, butcher knives and a sack of dried apples. The auctioneer seemed to have no guns. The miners stood around whittling and enjoying themselves.

"I got a bushel of neckties sent here by mistake, boys," said the Cheap John. "They'd fetch a dollar apiece back in the States. What'll you give me for the lot? Am I bid ten dollars? Am I bid nine dollars? Nine? Nine?"

The miners stood grinning and whittling and silent. At that moment Jimmie-from-Town spied Jack and Pitch-pine Billy.

"Let's go get something to eat," he said. "My stomach feels like a cat in Hades without claws."

"Nine, nine, nine," called the auctioneer.

"We've done," said Pitch-pine Billy.

"Done what?" asked Jimmie-from-Town, twisting the ends of his mustache hungrily.

"Ate," said Jack.

"*Eight*, eight, eight," called the auctioneer. "I'm bid

eight dollars by the young feller with yeller eyebrows. Sold for eight dollars."

Jack stood as if struck by lightning. The miners began to chuckle. "Looks like you bought yourself a bushel of neckties, Jamoka Jack," laughed Pitch-pine Billy.

"But I said *ate*—not eight," Jack protested.

"That's what I heard you say. *Eight*," answered the Cheap John, pushing the plug hat to the back of his head.

"A-t-e!"

"We ain't much on spellin' around here." It was clear to everyone that the auctioneer hadn't expected to be able to sell the ties at all. "You ain't going back on your word, are you?"

"Can't do that," whispered Pitch-pine Billy. "I'd rather see you break your leg than your word, boy. Pay up."

The auctioneer was grinning. "Why, you got them ties dirt cheap. Of course, we ain't much on tie-wearing here at the diggings—except to be buried in." And he burst out laughing.

The miners looked upon the affair as harmless fun. "Might be able to stuff a pillow with 'em," someone called out.

"Knot 'em together and lasso chickens."

Jack stepped up to the gold scale and pulled the

buckskin pouch from his belt. The nugget tumbled out. He borrowed a knife and carved half of it away, bit by bit. It hurt. He clamped his jaws with anger. Then he picked up the bushel of neckties and worked his way through the crowd to the street.

"Ain't so sure I'd even want to be *buried* in one of them things," a miner laughed.

Praiseworthy was coming along the street from the hotel and Jack could barely face him. He had cut two ounces off his nugget that might have gone toward their grubstake—or a gun. But even Pitch-pine Billy and Jimmie-from-Town were chuckling.

"What have you got there?" Praiseworthy asked, raising one eyebrow.

"Neckties," Jack murmured. "A whole bushel of them." Praiseworthy raised the other eyebrow.

"Neckties?"

"Yes, sir."

Jimmie-from-Town loosened his gold pouch. "I guess it was my fault," he smiled. "I'll pay you for them ties, Jamoka Jack, as long as you don't make me wear one."

"Me either," grinned Pitch-pine Billy.

Praiseworthy held up his hand. "Put away your dust." He looked at Jack. "That was a fine purchase," he smiled. "A brilliant purchase."

Jack gazed up at Praiseworthy. "What?"

"We'll buy our mountain canary with neckties."

Pitch-pine Billy crimped an eye. "You gone out of your head, Bullwhip? Why, you couldn't *give* them things away in Hangtown. The only necktie you can get on a man is made out of rope."

Praiseworthy scratched his short whiskers. They were at an itchy stage. He smiled, half shutting one eye. "Unless I miss my guess every man in the diggings will come begging for a necktie in a day or two. They'll fight to get one."

He picked up the bushel basket and swung it to his shoulder. "Come along, partner."

The next morning Praiseworthy and Jack helped Pitch-pine Billy dig a coyote hole.

"Once we hit bedrock there's no tellin' the riches down there," the miner declared. "The spangles keep workin' and siftin' through the ground. Earthquakes and all. It may take 'em ten thousand and one years to reach bedrock, but that stops 'em."

By late afternoon the big hole was deeper than Praiseworthy's head. They rigged up a rope and lifted out dirt by the bucketsful. There were men all along the diggings coyote-ing for gold and some of the shafts were as deep as wells.

Jack took his turns at the bottom of the hole, filling buckets that were emptied into the Long Tom. The Long Tom was a wooden sluice box set in the stream. Rushing water washed the dirt along a trough and the bits of gold were trapped in iron riffles along the bottom.

Praiseworthy kept silent about the neckties. Even by the end of the next day there was no rush to buy them, as he had predicted. But he remained unconcerned. Jack wondered if Praiseworthy had merely been trying to spare his feelings after the ridiculous purchase he'd made. He was glad to forget it, and said no more.

The following morning a delegation of three men appeared on Pitch-pine Billy's claim. Jack recognized Mr. Jonas T. Fletcher at once. The undertaker had brought two Hangtown merchants with him. They came looking for Praiseworthy, who was at the bottom of the coyote hole.

Jack and Pitch-pine Billy hauled him out on a rope and Praiseworthy looked as if he had been dipped in dust. It clung to his eyelashes as he blinked. "If bedrock's any deeper," he said to Pitch-pine Billy, "we'll be digging for gold in China."

"Bullwhip," said the undertaker. "You've got to uphold the fair name of Hangtown."

"What's that?"

"We've just been delivered a challenge."

Praiseworthy began beating the dirt out of his slouch hat. "It that so?"

"Yup. A fellow over at Grizzly Flats has heard about you. He says he can whip you."

Jack looked up. Praiseworthy hardly blinked an eye. He merely continued knocking the dust out of his hat. "Is that so?" he said.

"Yup. Of course, he don't know B from a bull's foot to make a statement like that. He ain't exactly bright, although I understand he can write his own name if you give him time enough. But he is a regular big fella. The Mountain Ox, they call him. Well, how about it?"

"It doesn't sound like a fair match," said Praiseworthy.

The undertaker nodded. "He does have you on height and weight and reach and general meanness, I suppose."

"That's not what I meant," said Praiseworthy. "It wouldn't be fair to *him*."

The three gentlemen from Hangtown responded with a blank look. "How's that?"

Even Jack was startled by Praiseworthy's declaration. The Mountain Ox sounded enormous. Praiseworthy wouldn't have a chance. Had he begun to believe his own reputation?

"From what you tell me, gentlemen," said Praiseworthy, "the man can barely read and write. He'll be at a decided disadvantage."

Pitch-pine Billy pulled his hat down over his ears. "Bullwhip, will you tell me what readin' and writin' has got to do with a bare-knuckle fightin' match?"

"I suppose that remains to be seen."

"Then you'll fight him?" the undertaker grinned.

"Not by choice, sir," said Praiseworthy. "But if the fair name of Hangtown is at stake, I suppose I must."

The delegation smiled. "How about next Tuesday?"

"Impossible. By next Tuesday we'll have our burro and grubstake and be far away prospecting. My partner and I have a fortune to make and time is running out. We'll be returning this way by the middle of August at the very latest. You can plan the match for the fifteenth, sir."

The three gentlemen from Hangtown nodded and departed. Jack gazed at Praiseworthy as if a complete stranger had been hiding through the years under the elegant manners of a butler. He was enchanted.

But Pitch-pine Billy whipped off his hat and jumped on it. "Bullwhip," he snorted, "you've gone and lost your reason. Before the fifteenth day of next month shows up— you better make out your last will and testament!"

* * *

Jack had just lowered himself into the coyote hole when a sudden excitement spread through the diggings, and he pulled himself out again. There was a shout of voices back and forth across the stream, from claim to claim.

"Ol' Quartz Jackson is back—and he's brought his new missus with him!"

Men dropped their shovels and gold pans and abandoned their Long Toms. Miners crawled out of coyote holes.

"What's that?"

"Him and the lady is puttin' up at the hotel!"

The excitement even touched Pitch-pine Billy. "Boys," he said to Praiseworthy and Jack, "I ain't seen a lady in so long I near forgot what they look like!"

Praiseworthy rested his arms on the handle of his shovel and grinned. He gave Jack a nod. "This is the day we've been waiting for, partner. Watch and see."

Pitch-pine Billy scowled. "Well, don't just stand there. Look at you both. Dirt stickin' out on you like you ain't had a bath all year. Why, it's a disgrace. I'm ashamed of you. You heard what they said—there's a lady in town."

Within five minutes miners were everywhere along the stream, scrubbing and shouting and planning to go to town. Pitch-pine Billy waded in with his clothes on and kept dumping hatloads of water over his head. Later, shirts and trousers could be seen on every bush, drying out in the mountain heat.

Men stood at mirrors tacked to trees and got out their straight razors. Half-a-dozen familiar beards disappeared. Others were trimmed and shortened.

Praiseworthy took his time. When he and Jack emerged from their canvas tent they were wearing bright green neckties. Pitch-pine Billy stood fluffing out his beard. He stopped and he stared.

"Help yourself," said Praiseworthy. "That is, if it's all right with my partner."

"It's fine with me," said Jack.

Pitch-pine Billy grinned. "Don't mind if I do."

The neckties were so bright they could be seen across the river. Soon the miners who had laughed at Jack the night of the auction were swarming about the bushel basket.

"I'll give you a pinch of dust for one of them neckties, Jamoka Jack."

"I'll give you *two* pinches."

Pitch-pine Billy was laughing. "Don't fight, boys. Just get in line there. Looks like Jamoka Jack has cornered the necktie market. He caught you sleepin', didn't he? Just hold your pouches open and I'll pinch out the gold—since I got the biggest thumbs in the diggin's."

Praiseworthy stood idly by with his foot on a stump and lit a Long Nine cigar. Within twenty minutes the basket was empty. Every necktie was gone. Pitch-pine Billy pulled the strings on Jack's buckskin pouch and handed it over. It was heavy as a plummet.

Jack weighed it in his hand and tossed the pouch to Praiseworthy. "That ought to get us a burro," he grinned.

"And maybe a gun," Praiseworthy said, taking the heft of it. He tossed the pouch back. "Yes sir, that Cheap John had better learn B from a bull's foot to get the better of Jamoka Jack. Gents, let's go to town."

The miners had formed a crowd outside the Empire Hotel and when Quartz Jackson brought his lady out onto the porch, the miners whipped off their hats as if it were the United States flag they were looking at.

"By the Great Horn Spoon," Pitch-pine Billy muttered in awe. "A genuine woman."

She had sparkling eyes and a smile for everyone. Quartz Jackson wore a vest with a watch chain across it and looked proud enough to burst.

"We freighted up some cut lumber," he said. "The missus and me, we're going to build a cabin and you boys are always welcome to drop in for tea. Ain't that right, Hanna?"

"Hanna," Pitch-pine Billy murmured. "Ain't that the pertiest name you ever heard?"

Quartz Jackson looked out over the crowd. He recognized Praiseworthy and Jack and gave them a nod. "Step up, boys, and I'll introduce you. Make it fast, before you strangle in them neckties!"

14 The Prospectors

WHEN JACK AWOKE the next morning he threw off his blanket and rushed outside to see if their burro was still there. It was. Tied to a stake outside the tent.

"Good morning, Stubb," Jack smiled.

Stubb was a veteran of the gold diggings. He gave Jack a haughty look. "Stubb's a proud animal," the man had said when they bought him. "Sometimes he thinks he's a mule." The burro's head seemed almost as large as his hindquarters and his dark ears stood up like the wings of a hawk. Jack liked him.

"We're going to be friends," he said. "Yes, sir."

He untied the burro and threw a leg over his back. Stubb kicked out his hind legs, his tail flew, and Jack hit the dirt. The burro turned his thick neck and peered at Jack with disdain. Jack was so surprised he just sat there.

"That wasn't very friendly," said Jack.

Pitch-pine Billy, standing in the opening of his dusty tent, roared out laughing. "You heard what the man said, Jamoka Jack. He said that mountain canary thinks he's a mule."

Jack brushed himself off. "All I wanted was to ride him."

Pitch-pine Billy pulled a red bandana out of his pocket and came over. "The mules in these hills is still half wild." He tied the handkerchief around Stubb's eyes. "They don't take kindly to bein' pack animals. You blindfold 'em first and they'll stand still."

Praiseworthy came out of the tent and stretched and sat on a stump to watch. Daylight was filtering through the trees and the morning had a fresh, piney smell.

Jack walked around the burro, sizing him up. Then he spit in his hands, threw a leg over Stubb's back and held on.

"Ready?" said Pitch-pine Billy.

"Ready," said Jack.

Pitch-pine Billy pulled off the bandana. Jack braced

himself. Stubb stood for a moment, as if trying to make up his mind whether to act like a mule or a burro.

"Good boy, Stubb," Jack said tentatively.

The burro flagged his ears and seemed satisfied that he had been shown the proper respect. He gave a little kick, just to get it out of his system, and behaved himself. Jack walked him up and back until breakfast was ready and slipped to the ground. "We got ourselves a good burro," he called to Praiseworthy.

Stubb gave a kick, as if in protest.

"Mule, I mean," Jack corrected himself.

After breakfast they struck the tent, blindfolded Stubb and cinched the wooden pack saddle to his back. They loaded up their grub and supplies, slipped their pick and shovel through the pack ropes and were ready to leave. Jimmie-from-Town came over with Buffalo John, both still wearing their neckties from the night before.

Pitch-pine Billy gazed out over the diggings. "Hangtown just won't be the same with a lady in it."

"Goodbye, gents," Praiseworthy said.

"I've a good mind to leave with you," scowled Pitch-pine Billy.

Other miners came over and it took five minutes to get their goodbyes said.

"We'll be lookin' for you back come the middle of next month," said Buffalo John. "You and the Mountain Ox."

"I'll be here," Praiseworthy said, taking the blindfold off Stub's face. "Let's get going, partner."

Praiseworthy picked up their new squirrel gun and Jack took Stub's rope. The squirrel gun wasn't what Jack had had in mind, like a four-shooter, but it would do. They'd be able to hunt a little game and he supposed it would stand off an outlaw or two if they met up with any.

In jackboots and red shirts, they began walking upstream and soon the farewell shouts of their friends were lost in the trees. It was a fine morning to be going prospecting, but Jack found it hard to walk away from Pitch-pine Billy and Jimmie-from-Town and even Buffalo John. Still, coming back would be even harder.

"Maybe the Mountain Ox isn't as big and terrible as they say he is," Jack murmured.

"Worse, no doubt," said Praiseworthy. He sounded positively light-hearted.

"Are you really going to come back and fight him?"

"I gave my word, didn't I?"

"Bare-knuckle?"

"Absolutely." Praiseworthy was not pleased that he had won his name and reputation because he had swung on a road agent with a weighted glove.

Jack kept a grip on Stubb's rope and the animal followed with a clanging of drinking cups, coffee pot, gold pans and empty tin cans. Jack had a sudden vision of his partner lying in the dust of the street, beaten and humiliated. "Most of the miners are betting on the Mountain Ox," he muttered.

Praiseworthy scratched through his whiskers. "I know that. But I intend to beat him."

"With reading and writing?"

"Exactly." Praiseworthy pushed the slouch hat back on his head. "Miss Arabella once asked me to destroy a book she found in your grandfather's library. If I remember correctly it was called *The Gentleman's Book of Boxing, or The Fine Art of Fisticuffs Explained and Illustrated*—she was afraid it might fall into your hands, I suppose. I don't mind telling you that I didn't destroy it. I read it. I devoured it. Fascinating. I believe I could recite whole pages to you. Now it stands to reason that the Mountain Ox has never read a book in his life. He's no doubt a mere brawler. Therefore, since I have outread him, I see no reason why I cannot outwit and outbox him. To be perfectly honest with you—I'm beginning to look forward to it."

The two partners exchanged a glance and a smile and continued on their way. Jack put the Mountain Ox out of his mind.

"Do you want to carry our gun?" said Praiseworthy.

"I'd like to carry our gun," said Jack. He took it in the crook of his arm, while Praiseworthy led the burro, and kept an eye out for rabbits, squirrels, savages and outlaws. All they had to do now was find pay dirt.

15 The Man Who Couldn't Sit Down

THEY PITCHED CAMP and they broke camp. Day after day they followed running water. They washed out "prospects" scraped from behind rocks and boulders in the stream bed. Spangles had a way of trapping themselves out of the current.

When they found bits of color, they dug in. At times Praiseworthy spent the entire day with his boots apart, swinging the pick in great arcs. Where the prospects looked good they labored to follow the specks of gold to their source, which either disappeared or ended at some-one's claim.

Where the fleas were bad at night they stuck a lit candle in the floor of the tent and in the morning Jack would count the visitors to see whose gold pan had trapped the most. He kept track.

"I'm ahead by eighty-two dead varmints," he announced at the end of their first week of prospecting.

"And I've got the live varmint bites to prove it," Praiseworthy answered, scratching his back.

The days were long and hot. Yellow poppies had burst open on the hillsides like scatterings of fools' gold. Sometimes Jack would catch Praiseworthy gazing out over some distant view as if it didn't matter if they ever got back to Boston.

"Smell that air, partner," Praiseworthy would say, as if mountain air had just been discovered.

Pay dirt eluded them—but the next bend in the river might make their fortune. They met other prospectors every day and at times there seemed to be more pack mules and burros in the hills than jackrabbits.

After supper one night, Praiseworthy and Jack sat around their coffee fire and a miner came along on muleback.

"Have a cup," said Praiseworthy, smoking one of the Long Nine cigars he had taken a fancy to.

"Can't stop," said the miner as if he had a mouthful of

gravel. A bandana was tied around his face and one cheek was swelled out. "Got a powerful toothache. Much obliged, anyhow."

"Where you heading?"

"Over to Shirt-tail Camp. I hear they got a tooth extractor up there."

Jack pricked up his ears. Praiseworthy lowered his eyebrows. "Would his name be Higgins?"

"Doc Higgins, that's him." The miner gave his mule a small kick with his heels and was gone.

Jack shook his head. "I hope I don't get a toothache. No, sir."

"The imposter!" Praiseworthy snapped. "So that's where he ran off to. Cut-Eye Higgins, dentist—of Shirt-tail Camp. No doubt he extracts teeth and gold pouches at the same time."

The days passed in sweat and hard labor. The two partners kept on the move, looking for a claim to stake. They passed from ravine to ravine. The findings were slim. Still, Praiseworthy sang as he swung the pick and Jack whistled a great deal. They got used to the sight of Digger Indians. The women, in bright calico dresses, would come to the edge of the stream to pan in tightly woven flat baskets. The gold fever had passed no one by.

"Oh, it ain't gold fever the Diggers has got," a prospector told them. "The yellow stuff don't mean a thing to them. It's calico fever them ladies has got. And the men, they got serape fever and red sash fever. That's what they trade their dust for, poor devils. They do like to dress up, don't they? Like a bunch of young'uns."

Stubb caused them no trouble, as long as they treated him with the respect due a mule. Slowly, Praiseworthy and Jack added dust to their gold pouches, but they were as far as ever from striking it rich. Here and there could be seen mounds of dirt and coyote holes where other miners had tried their luck. They passed through abandoned camps where Chinese had moved in to sift through the diggings left behind by others. And they always seemed to be finding color that had escaped the pans and Long Toms and rockers that had come before them.

Jack had seen rockers made out of anything from provision boxes to hollowed out logs. When finished, they had the look of cradles. You shoveled dirt into a hopper at the top, added water and rocked the spangles through to riffles in the bottom. Men could be found on almost every claim rocking the cradle, like grizzled nursemaids.

Jack was fond of carrying the squirrel gun. They had been shooting what small game they could, especially after their bacon gave out. One afternoon, late in July, after they had made camp, it seemed to Jack that he couldn't face another plate of beans. He picked up the squirrel gun. "I'm going to hunt us a jackrabbit for dinner," he declared.

"I can't imagine anything that would taste better," said Praiseworthy, chewing on a piece of oat straw.

"I'll be back."

"I'll expect you."

Jack wandered off, with the gun in the crook of his arm. He could feel new muscles along his shoulders and his legs had a spring to them. If Aunt Arabella and his sisters could see him now, he thought. They'd faint away, one, two, three. He stopped to take aim at a mountain cat he imagined crouched on the limb of a tree. Bam! He'd skin it and make himself a hat.

The sun was setting and the sky turned red. He raised a pair of gray doves, but he didn't have the heart to shoot them. They flew off making a sound as if their wings squeaked. High in the trees carpentaros were hammering away with their beaks. Not woodpeckers, he imagined himself explaining to Constance and Sarah. We call 'em carpentaros in the diggings.

Praiseworthy took advantage of Jack's absence to try a little shadow boxing. He turned the pages of the book over in his mind. *Elbows in. Left jab. Feint. Duck, sir, duck. Now the right. Put your shoulder to it, sir!*

The sky began to darken and Jack was unable to flush a rabbit. Instead, he flushed a grizzly bear.

The great furry beast came crashing out of the shadows. He stopped, seeing Jack for the first time. Jack stood instantly petrified. He felt as if his boots were suddenly nailed to the ground. Twenty yards away stood a grizzly and all he had was a squirrel gun. The animal rose on its hind legs and showed his teeth in a warning snarl.

Jack tried to remember the things Mountain Jim had once told him about trapping grizzlies. But he didn't have a trap. He just had the squirrel gun. And the brute would brush off squirrel shot like so many flies. The grizzly opened his mouth wider, dropping some half-chewed acorns, and roared. I'm done for, Jack thought. Done for.

He got his feet to move. He began to back up. Light was fading quickly. The grizzly dropped to all fours and came rolling forward. And then he stopped, for Jack had suddenly disappeared from the face of the earth.

He had fallen down a coyote hole.

Squirrel gun and all.

The bear went up on his hind legs again and peered everywhere. He snarled. He roared. Jack waited twenty feet down, afraid the grizzly would fall in on him. Then the sound of the carpentaros burying acorns caught the beast's attention. He went crashing away to go climb a tree.

Jack was scraped and bruised, but had broken no bones. It was only after he tried to climb out of the hole that he realized he might be late for supper.

He couldn't get out.

The sheer earthen walls gave way at every hand and foot hold. Once he got himself halfway to the top, only to tumble to the bottom with a small avalanche of loose dirt. He began to call out, even though camp was too far away for Praiseworthy to hear him. He shouted anyway and waited and shouted again.

Finally he took aim at the dusky sky and fired. The explosion boomed like a cannon and earth rained in on him. When the dust cleared a face appeared overhead.

"Help, sir!" Jack said.

"What are you doin' down there?"

"Trying to get out, sir!"

"I heard you callin'. You almost shot my hat off."

"Sorry, sir."

"I'll throw you a rope."

After a moment the rope tumbled in on Jack. He took

a firm grip, hung onto the squirrel gun and the stranger pulled him out.

Jack planted his feet on solid ground and heaved a sigh of relief. He was dirt from head to toe. "I'm obliged, sir," he smiled.

"Why, you're just a lad," the man said, coiling the rope and hanging it on the saddle of his horse.

And then Jack took a look at the stranger. He was a big man with worn boots and a white coat. A white linen coat. Cut-Eye Higgins's coat!

Jack backed away, almost stepping into the coyote hole again.

"What's the matter, boy? You look like you seen ol' Scratch himself."

Jack's heart was pounding. "I know who you are— you're a road agent!"

"Now, that's a fact," the man laughed. "But I've retired from the road agent profession. That's fact, too. The boys was all shot, hung or lost their ears. I got away with a load of buckshot in the seat of my pants. Why, I ain't been able to sit down in a month. Me and my horse, we both walk and hunt grizzlies. I'm reformed, that's a fact. You ain't seen a big fella around here, have you? I been on his tracks for two days."

Jack got a grip on himself, but he kept his distance. "I'll bet you're still out hunting for Dr. Buckbee's mine."

"Mine? What mine is that, boy?"

Jack blinked. Didn't he know? Hadn't he ripped open the lining of Cut-Eye Higgins's coat? Jack found himself leveling the squirrel gun.

"You pointin' that thing at me?" the reformed road agent laughed.

"Yes, sir."

"Now, that's no way to treat your benefactor, is it?"

"You stole that coat you're wearing, didn't you?"

"I reckon I did. Belong to a friend of yours? Why, it gives me a bad conscience to wear this coat—although I was awful fond of it. I'd appreciate it if you'd give it back. Always was too tight on me anyway."

He peeled off the linen coat and threw it toward Jack. Jack let it lie on the ground even though he could hardly wait to get his hands on it. The map must still be sewn up in the lining!

The man took the halter of his horse. "Now if you'll just let me walk away without shootin'," he smiled, "I'll be obliged. Sure you ain't seen a big grizzly around? With the price they're payin' for bear steaks, he's almost worth his weight in gold."

"He just left," said Jack.

"Then I'll be goin'." The ex-highwayman started away and then turned with a final laugh. "Boy, the next time you point that squirrel gun at a bad hombre like me, you really ought to trouble yourself to reload it first. Good luck, boy."

Jack's face reddened under the layers of dust. He watched the man disappear through the trees. He was sorry he hadn't been more polite to his benefactor. "Thank you, sir!" he called.

Praiseworthy was just getting up to look for his partner when Jack burst into camp.

"Look what I've got!"

Praiseworthy peered at the white bundle Jack had made of the coat. "If that's a rabbit, I'll eat beans."

"It's Cut-Eye Higgins's coat."

Jack quickly told of meeting up with the grizzly, falling into a coyote hole and being pulled out by the reformed road agent. Just as quickly Praiseworthy unclasped his knife and ripped open the lining. They laid open every inch of the coat. They examined and re-examined it, and Jack's excitement died away. There was no map. There had never been a map sewn in the lining of the coat.

"The scoundrel deceived us," Praiseworthy muttered.

"He never lost the map to those highwaymen. It has no doubt taken him to Shirt-tail Camp and he may not have located the mine even yet. Otherwise, he wouldn't bother to pull teeth. Put some beans on to fry, partner Jack. First thing in the morning we'll start for Shirt-tail Camp."

16 The Gravediggers

THEY WERE TWO days finding their way to Shirttail Camp. They followed the South Fork of the American River into the winding Coloma Valley. The summer hills were red and yellow. They passed within ten feet of Old Cap Sutter's sawmill. Jack heard everyone in the diggings refer to Sutter as Old Cap and he knew the miners' yarns about the sawmill. He looked at it now—a rough, timbered shack on stilts at the water's edge.

Old Cap had hired a carpenter named Jim Marshall to build it—that was the way the yarn began. On a chill January morning in '48 the carpenter spied a yellow glitter in the tailrace. He thought it might be fool's gold until he beat it with a rock. That was the test. Fool's gold was brittle and would splinter. Real gold was soft and would flatten out.

The lump flattened out like a yellow button.

Marshall rushed off to Sacramento, where Old Cap had built a fort, and arrived in a pouring rain with the news. He made Old Cap bolt the door, pulled a white cotton rag from a pocket of his wet pantaloons and revealed his discovery. Jim Marshall was so excited he could barely speak.

The two men tried other tests. They got bowls of water and a scale. Using an equal amount of silver, they weighed the two metals under water. The gold was heavier. Then they tested the samples with acid to see if they would corrode. They wouldn't. There was no longer any question about Marshall's discovery in the tailrace. He had found gold. The news leaked out—and the rush for yellow treasure began. Squatters came swarming into the valley and now a town had sprung up on both sides of the river. Jack had never seen so many Long Toms and rockers in his life.

"Is this the way to Shirt-tail Camp?" Praiseworthy asked a miner standing knee-deep in water and mud.

"Just follow the river. If you hurry you might get there

in time for the hangin'. A lot of the boys has taken the day off for the festivites."

Praiseworthy shrugged. "We're in no hurry, my partner and I."

"It's that dentist fella. They caught him trying to run off on a stolen horse."

Praiseworthy and Jack exchanged a quick glance. The map. Only Cut-Eye Higgins knew where Dr. Buckbee's gold bonanza might be. He couldn't talk very well hanging from a limb, much as he deserved it, no doubt.

"On second thought," said Praiseworthy, "we're in a terrible hurry. Good day, sir."

They arrived at Shirt-tail Camp in an hour. It was a dusty village of round tents and square tents and plank shacks roofed with pine boughs.

"There," said Jack, "there he is!"

He saw Cut-Eye Higgins seated on a horse under the limb of a tree. He wore his jipijapa hat and around his neck, a noose. The scar across his eye set his face at a hard squint. A crowd was ringed around him.

"We're just in time," Jack murmured.

Praiseworthy whipped out Stubb's red bandana blindfold and quickly tied it around Jack's face. "Partner, you've got a toothache."

"What?"

"Moan now and then. Good and loud. Come on."

Jack gulped and followed Praiseworthy through the crowd. A paunchy man with a curly fringe of whiskers from ear to ear seemed to be in charge of festivities. "Doc," he was saying, "you know the verdict of the jury. As Justice of the Peace of Shirt-tail Camp I'll see you get a good buryin' as befits a professional man such as yourself. We don't mind so much that you extracted a gold pouch every time we opened our mouths. There's plenty of yeller around. And that you light-fingered every pocket watch in town so that nobody knows what time it is. You're a professional man and we tried to make allowances. But horse stealin' is a heinous crime and you got to pay the penalty. Since you said your last words two-three times already this afternoon, let's get on with it. Boys, switch that horse."

"Hold on!" demanded Praiseworthy, stepping forward. "I've got a lad here with a powerful toothache."

The Justice of the Peace threw down his hat. "Doggone! That's the third one today. We'll never get him strung up."

"I beg of you, gents," said Praiseworthy. "We've come a long way and it'll only take a moment. The boy is in pain. Listen to him moan."

Jack bellowed and held a hand to his cheek. He wasn't

pretending. He was downright scared they might let Cut-Eye Higgins pull one of his teeth.

"All right," said the chin-whiskered official. "Get the doc down off that horse. Hiram, give him back his forceps and bring that molasses barrel for the boy to sit on."

Jack moaned again and watched the men help Cut-Eye Higgins off the saddle. He seemed a little weak in the knees. They cut the rope binding his wrists behind his back, but left the noose around his neck. He peered from Jack to Praiseworthy. It was a moment before he recognized the butler in red shirt, jackboots and whiskers.

"Never thought I'd be glad to see *you* again," he said. His face was pale and his usual sneer was gone. Reluctantly, Jack seated himself on the molasses barrel and the doomed man clapped an eye on him. "Open your mouth, son, and stop squirming."

Jack took one look at the steel forceps in Cut-Eye Higgins's shaky hand and decided that a team of mules wasn't going to get his mouth open.

"Let's see them ivories," Cut-Eye Higgins said under his breath. "I'll just tinker—you didn't come to me to have any yanked."

"We came for the map," Praiseworthy muttered.

"I figured. Get me out of this and the map is yours."

Praiseworthy nodded. "It's a bargain. I'll do the best I can. But first, the map. I don't trust you even with a noose around your neck."

Cut-Eye Higgins lifted off his jipijapa hat and fished a thick, folded strip of brown paper out of the sweatband. It was as if he kept it there only to make his hat fit. When he returned the hat to his head it slipped down almost to his ears. "There's my part of the bargain. Now you keep yours. Open them jaws, boy."

Jack swallowed hard and opened up. The crowd watched and waited. Cut-Eye Higgins wiped the forceps on his sleeve and set to work. Praiseworthy opened up the folds of brown paper, studied the markings and within seconds he saw that the foxy scoundrel had out-foxed him again. The map traced a line along the North Fork of the American River, through the Coloma Valley and ended with an X-mark that could only be Shirt-tail Camp.

"Why, this map is no good," snapped Praiseworthy.

"I didn't say it was. Except to make my hat fit. But that's the map Buckbee's brother made before he died. The same. The genuine article. Only in the meantime them pockets of gold got discovered *all over again*. By time I got here there were a hundred miners on the spot."

Jack moaned as best he could with the forceps trying

to spread his teeth apart. Their fifty-fifty share of Dr. Buckbee's mine was worthless. Cut-Eye Higgins had led them on a wild goose chase.

"Get me out of this noose," said Cut-Eye Higgins. "That was our bargain, wasn't it?"

Praiseworthy ripped the map to bits. He'd given his word and he had to stand by it.

"Gentlemen," he said, turning to the Justice of the Peace and others grouped around him. "I take it you have acted as judge and jury in this case."

"That's right," answered the official. "He got a fair trial and anyway, he was caught red-handed."

"Was he represented by counsel?"

"What for? We knew he was guilty."

"Under what law do you intend to dispatch Doc Higgins from the limb of that tree?"

"Why, everybody knows horse stealin' is agin the law."

"What law?"

"Now listen here, stranger. There ain't a law book within fifty miles that I know of. I hear they had one over at Growlersburg, but it was printed on thin paper and the boys took to rollin' cigarettes with it. Speakin' for myself, I don't see any reason to let law interfere with justice around here. We never did before."

Praiseworthy began pacing slowly back and forth. "In

the absence of book law, gentlemen, I recommend to your notice that humanity is also lacking in this case. You're about to string up the only dentist in these diggings. Is that human? He may deserve his fate, but what of the innocent whose only crime is to come down with the toothache?" Praiseworthy turned and made a grand, court-room gesture toward Jack. "Like my young partner there. Think of the pain and suffering you will inflict on those in dire need of a tooth extractor. Tomorrow it may be you, sir, with your cheek swelled up like a melon. Or you, sir, Mr. Justice of the Peace, with a pain in your jaw as if you had a bee for a molar stinging away from morning till night."

One by one, he singled out the gentlemen of the jury and one by one they found themselves rubbing their jaws as if they could almost feel a toothache coming on. Praise-worthy had never made a speech in his life, but the words rolled off his tongue and he could feel their effect on the crowd. When he finished he was greeted with a yell of approval.

"He's talkin' sense," someone called out.

"The doc can't pull teeth if he's six feet under."

"We could put him in jail."

The Justice of Shirt-tail Camp shook his head. "Boys, we ain't got a jail. You know that. The verdict was string

177

him up, but I suppose I could delay sentence. Until another tooth extractor shows up in these parts. There's bound to be one before long. *Then* we'll get on with the sentence."

There was general approval from the crowd, and two toothaches broke out on the spot. Praiseworthy was astonished by the power he had found in his voice. The two miners got in line at the molasses barrel and Jack was glad to give up his place.

"My tooth has stopped hurting," he said and Cut-Eye Higgins gave him a wink with his bad eye.

"Doc Higgins," said the Justice of the Peace, "you got yourself a temporary reprieve. When you finish with them extractin' jobs you stand still and we're going to build a jail house around you. There'll be visitin' hours for anyone with the toothache. But I'll see you hung yet—and soon as possible." Then he turned to Praiseworthy. "Stranger, I promised the Doc a good buryin' befittin' a professional man. Might as well get all in readiness. Since you appointed yourself counsel for the defense you get up in the hills and dig him a restin' place. Make it six feet deep."

"Why six feet?"

"Don't be cantankerous or I'll fine you for bein' in contempt of court. Everybody knows a grave has got to be six feet deep. Get goin'."

The two partners returned to their burro and led him into the hills above the diggings. "You sure made a good speech," Jack said. "It was something to hear. A regular lawyer couldn't have done better. And you saved Cut-Eye Higgins from being strung up."

"It's just temporary—which is about all he deserves."

They chose a bare spot about half a mile from camp. It was on a bluff covered with oat straw and overlooking the river. They pulled pick and shovel from Stubb's pack ropes and set to work.

"Fine-looking country, isn't it?" Praiseworthy muttered. "Even to be buried in."

Jack tried not to think about Boston. It would soon be time to start back and all they had to show for their labors was a worthless map. Poor Aunt Arabella, he thought. They would lose the house for sure. The entire trip to California was beginning to look like a wild-goose chase.

When they got the hole four feet deep they couldn't go any farther. They hit bedrock.

And struck gold.

JACK VERY NEARLY jumped a foot. "By the Great Horn Spoon!" he yelled. "Look!"

"I see it!"

"Pay dirt!"

And Praiseworthy exclaimed, "Yeller as can be!"

The gold revealed itself like bits of sunlight trapped in the loosened earth. The two partners flung their hats in the air. In sheer exuberance they clasped arms and swung around and around in the oblong pit.

"We've done it, Jack, we've done it!" Praiseworthy roared.

"We've struck it rich!"

It was a moment before Jack, in his excitement, realized that Praiseworthy had called him *Jack*. Not Master Jack. Just Jack. Plain Jack—the way he'd always wanted it to be! He thought he'd never stop leaping for joy, but then he fished out a golden lump and beat it with a stone. "Flat as a button!"

"Cut some stakes—quick, Jack."

Anything would do. Praiseworthy drew his tattered umbrella from their pack and pounded it into the ground. it made a fine corner post for their claim. Jack stripped a fallen pine limb with their clasp knife. Praiseworthy measured out fifty feet, by strides, which would give them plenty of elbow room. Soon they had the boundaries staked and Jack ran from corner to corner hanging tin cans in place. They had their claim, legal as could be.

And Praiseworthy laughed, "Cut-Eye Higgins has done us a good turn—in spite of himself!"

After the first day's washings Praiseworthy went to Coloma to buy a Long Tom and Jack stayed behind with the squirrel gun to keep an eye on things. Within twenty-four hours miners had staked claims everywhere around them. The place quickly got the name of Gravediggers' Hill.

Praiseworthy and Jack worked from morning till night. They carried pay dirt bucket by bucket down the slope to the sluice box in the river. The hole grew wider and longer. They filled a buckskin pouch and tied it off at the top. Hour after hour Praiseworthy swung the pick and day after day Jack emptied bucket after bucket into the Long Tom. Their fortune grew heavier.

"Won't Aunt Arabella be surprised when we walk in," Jack grinned one night after supper. Praiseworthy was smoking one of his Long Nine cigars. "Why, we'll be able to use sacks of gold for doorstops!"

Praiseworthy gazed into the coffee fire and his fingers touched Miss Arabella's small portrait buttoned in the pocket of his shirt. She was so far away, a continent away, in Boston. He wondered what she was doing at that very moment. Staring into the fireplace and thinking of him, perhaps. But that was nonsense, he told himself quickly, and turned from the fire. He must not forget his place.

Once back in Boston he would take up his old duties again. He was, he reminded himself firmly, born and bred a butler—like his father before him, and *his* father before him. Miss Arabella would be lost without him. Why, Boston would never accept him as anything but what he was— a butler. Still, Boston was a long way off and there was the sound of the river below to enjoy and the cigar between his teeth to savor.

One morning a miner came rushing up the hill from Shirt-tail Camp. "Doc Higgins has escaped!"

"What's that?" said Praiseworthy, dropping his pick.

"Yup. During the night. He used them forceps of his on the jail house we built. Pulled the nails through like he was yankin' teeth and got a board loose. Slipped right out. He's long gone by now and good riddance."

Praiseworthy wiped the sweat that had rolled down into his whiskers. "Maybe he learned a lesson, but I doubt it. He's just running from one noose to another. There are plenty of hanging trees in the diggings and he'll be standing under one, sooner or later, with his feet off the ground."

After almost two weeks of busting ground and shoveling dirt their claim began to play itself out. The washings grew thinner and thinner. One by one the other miners gave up on Gravediggers' Hill. It had boomed and now it was dying. The boomers pulled their stakes to follow rumors of some other gold strike.

On the morning of the fifteenth of August, the day Praiseworthy was to face the Mountain Ox in bare-fisted combat, the two partners struck their tent. Praiseworthy seemed in no hurry to keep his appointment in Hangtown. Jack wondered if Praiseworthy had changed his mind.

"Not on your life, Jack. We'll make it."

Jack blindfolded Stubb and they loaded up. They had eleven heavy pouches of gold dust—worth a fortune in San Francisco.

"Providing we get it there," mused Praiseworthy.

"We might meet up with road agents again."

"Exactly. This squirrel gun of ours barely scares off squirrels. Jack, I think the time has come for shooting irons."

Jack's heart took a leap. "A four-shooter?"

"I think a four-shooter would be an excellent choice."

They stood for a last moment gazing at their claim. The umbrella still rose from a corner with a tin can on top. Praiseworthy left it there. Gravediggers' Hill had been good to them and they walked away as if they were abandoning an old friend. Almost at once several Chinese miners, with pigtails dangling from their flat straw hats, moved in to work over the diggings.

"Good luck, boys!" Praiseworthy called.

At Coloma they traded in their pick and shovel, tent and gold pans. They wouldn't be needing them any more.

They left Coloma on the stage, each with a revolver tucked in his belt. Jack rubbed his hand along the butt of the four-shooter. He felt invincible.

He turned for a last look at Stubb. They had sold him to the Justice of the Peace and at that moment the official was sitting in the dust, his legs spread out before him. The burro stood looking very pleased with himself.

"I forgot to tell him Stubb thinks he's a mule," said Jack.

Praiseworthy smiled. "I'd say the Justice of the Peace just found that out for himself."

They reached Hangtown late in the afternoon. The main street was hung with bunting as if it were the Fourth of July. The place swarmed with miners, horses, mules and burros. It looked to Jack as if every man and animal in the diggings had come to town.

When Praiseworthy stepped out of the stagecoach a shout went up.

"There he is! It's Bullwhip himself!"

Pitch-pine Billy rushed over with his ears bent under the weight of his hat. "It's about time," he spit. "The boys was grumblin' that you run out on the match—not that they blame you. Howdy, Jamoka Jack."

"Howdy, Pitch-pine Billy."

In another moment Jimmie-from-Town had crowded around, and Buffalo John and Quartz Jackson.

"You'll have to excuse the missus," said Quartz Jackson. "She don't want to watch."

"Let's get on with it," said Pitch-pine Billy. "Where's the Mountain Ox?"

"Eatin' oysters over at the Chinese chow chow," someone answered. "He got hungry waitin' around."

"Somebody fetch him. Boys, spread out."

The miners formed a large circle in the center of the street. Others climbed on the roofs of the stores for a better view. When the Mountain Ox appeared at the doorway of the Chinese restaurant, Jack's heart dropped to his boots.

The man from Grizzly Flats grinned. He had a neck like the stump of a tree. There was oyster juice in his beard. His chest looked as big around as a flour barrel.

"He is a large gent at that," said Praiseworthy studying his opponent at a distance. He handed Jack his revolver together with the buckskin pouches tucked under his belt and weighting down his pockets.

"I wish we'd never come back here," Jack muttered. "It's—it's not a fair match, no sir."

"You want me to back out?"

Jack took a breath, and shook his head. "You gave your word. You have got to stick by it."

"That's right. And anyway, I intend to lick him."

Praiseworthy stripped off his shirt. The Mountain Ox, across the way, did the same. He was hairy as a grizzly bear—and looked twice as broad.

Jonas T. Fletcher, the undertaker, stood in the clearing. "You two gladiators ready?"

Praiseworthy nodded.

The Mountain Ox wiped the juice from his beard. He grinned and turned to a Chinese in the crowd. "Ah Lee, go fry me up about two dozen more oysters. I'll be there in a minute—soon as I whip this Bullwhip fella."

"Come out fightin'," said the town undertaker. "If either one of you gets killed I'll give him a free funeral job. May the best man survive."

The undertaker scurried out of the clearing. Praiseworthy stepped forward, striking a pose with his arms. Elbows in, he told himself. The Mountain Ox came out with his arms spread like the wings of a buzzard.

The crowd stood tense. Squirts of chewing tobacco raised silent puffs of dust. Jack's heart was pounding in his ears. The gladiators closed the distance between them and the pride of Grizzly Flats wasted no time. He swung an arm with enough power to bust through a barn door. When it had run its course, the crowd was astonished to see Praiseworthy still standing. He had felt nothing more than the wind. He had ducked with the greatest of ease. The street brawler, with his wide open stance, signaled his punches in advance.

Immediately, Praiseworthy countered with a left jab. It didn't amount to much, but it surprised the Mountain Ox.

Jack gazed toward the center of the clearing with a leap of hope. In the afternoon heat Praiseworthy's back glistened with sweat. The new muscles along his arms and shoulders looked polished. Almost two months in the diggings, swinging a pick from morning till night, had had their effect. He had the power to bust through a barn door himself.

"Come on, Ox—finish him off!"

"Don't be scared of him, Bullwhip!"

Again the Mountain Ox swung and again Praiseworthy escaped with nothing more than a wind burn. He was getting the hang of it. He was vigilant. He concentrated. He knew that one misstep, one miscalculation, and the Mountain Ox would end the match with a single blow.

Five minutes passed. To Jack it was five hours, five days. The Mountain Ox swung one haymaker after the other, but Praiseworthy dodged, ducked or stepped aside. He cut a tall, lithe figure in the afternoon dust.

Having by now made a thorough study of his opponent, as the book advised, Praiseworthy devised his attack. Left jab, left jab, he told himself. Keep them coming like bee stings. To the proboscis. The Mountain Ox may be all muscle, but a nose is a nose.

The crowd, in growing amazement, watched and chewed tobacco and squirted juice. Not only was Praiseworthy still on his feet, he hadn't been touched.

The oysters in the Chinese chow chow burned to a crisp. Praiseworthy kept jabbing with his left, and the Mountain Ox's nose turned as round and red as a tomato. Once, when the gladiators had worked themselves to the very edge of the crowd, the Mountain Ox let fly a carefully aimed wallop. Just as carefully Praiseworthy ducked and the blow collided with Cheap John, the auctioneer. He went flying backwards, knocking down six miners like so many dominoes.

The bout continued without letup and the sun began to set through the pines. Praiseworthy had hardly exerted himself. He would duck, dispatch a left jab and resume the stance he remembered so well from *The Gentleman's Book of Boxing*. But the Mountain Ox had been swinging his arms like a windmill and now his tongue was very nearly hanging out. His brawler's arms, once so wide, he now seemed to drag at his sides. But like a wounded animal, he was still dangerous. Still, it seemed to Praiseworthy, the time had come to close the book. Big as was the pride of Grizzly Flats he had a jaw like other men, and a jaw was a jaw.

A final bee sting. The Mountain Ox shook his head and stuck out his jaw in fury. Praiseworthy stepped in with a right cross—from the shoulder, exactly as the book advised—and it felt to him as if he were hitting a barn door.

Jack held his breath. The Mountain Ox was still on his feet five seconds later. But then he keeled over backwards like a statue, and lay spread-eagled in the dust.

A roar burst from the crowd and Pitch-pine Billy rushed in to hold up Praiseworthy's arm. "The winner! I don't know how he done it—but you saw it! The fair name of Hangtown has been saved! Boys, let's celebrate!"

Praiseworthy pulled on his shirt and Jack handed him his revolver. He stuck it in his belt. The miners were raising noise all around them, but the two partners regarded each other, exchanging a silence. Finally Praiseworthy said, "How was that, Jack? I backed up my reputation fair and square, didn't I?"

Jack's face glowed as if he'd swallowed a lantern. He

was bursting with pride. There wasn't a man in the diggings he'd rather have for a partner—not Pitch-pine Billy or Quartz Jackson or Jimmie-from-Town or Buffalo John. "It wasn't a fair match, no sir," Jack grinned. "The Mountain Ox can hardly read or write. Why, he doesn't know B from a bull's foot."

18 Arrival at the Long Wharf

THE FOLLOWING MORNING Praiseworthy and Jack climbed aboard the stage for Sacramento City and were given a rousing send-off. Time was running out. Now that they had struck it rich they had better hurry back to Boston before Aunt Arabella sold the house with all its family memories.

But lately Praiseworthy found himself thinking less and less about Boston and more and more of Miss Arabella. She would like California, he thought; and of course, she ought to be finding herself a husband. A man would be lucky to have her at his side. If only he weren't a butler—

but that was unthinkable. He quickly forced the thought out of his head.

Jack was almost disappointed when they came down out of the mountains and arrived in Sacramento City without even a glimpse of a road agent. He had been ready at any moment to draw his four-shooter.

A steamboat was waiting in the river. They bought tickets and went aboard with their heavy pouches of gold dust. Sacramento City drifted away behind them and in fourteen hours they would be in San Francisco. The captain, they learned, was trying to break his own speed record.

"Fourteen hours *or less*," he chuckled from the pilot-house window. "Gentlemen, hold onto your hats!"

The small stern-wheeler went charging down the river, blasting its whistle at anything that got in its way—even floating logs. Kanaka sailors kept pitching cord wood into the furnace and on deck the passengers amused themselves watching the needle rise on the steam gauge.

"Forty-five pounds pressure and still risin'," a miner from Poverty Hill chuckled. "Why, we'll trim a full hour off the river record if we don't climb up on a sand bar first."

Another passenger shook his head. "It seems to me we could use a little less steam and a little more caution."

Praiseworthy and Jack were weighted down with treasure. They carried their pouches of gold dust securely tied
to their belts with their revolvers bristling in the sun.
Praiseworthy lit a Long Nine cigar and they sat behind
the jackstaff watching every bend in the river approach.

"Fine-looking country," Praiseworthy would say from
time to time.

"Fine-looking country," Jack would agree. He sensed
how much his partner hated to leave this rough, untamed
territory. No one in Boston would think of referring to
Praiseworthy as Bullwhip and Aunt Arabella would put a
stop to Jack's coffee drinking. But Boston was where they
belonged.

They were not the only miners aboard who were heading for home. They met passengers who had abandoned
the diggings in disgust, as poor as when they had arrived.
Some, standing for months in the chill streams, had
picked up nothing but the rheumatism. Still others, like
Praiseworthy and Jack, had struck it rich and their belts
and pockets were heavy with gold pouches.

The two partners slept in everything but their boots.
When they awoke the next morning and went out on deck
the stern-wheeler was entering the broad, blue stretches of
San Francisco Bay. The masts of hundreds of ships could
be seen in the distance, clustered around the port.

"We might get ourselves passage home today," said Jack.

"Might," said Praiseworthy. "Every day counts. We've got to reach Boston before Miss Arabella does anything foolish."

The passengers were gathering around the steam gauge again and someone called out, "Fifty-eight pounds pressure!"

"And still risin'!"

At that moment, with the Long Wharf less than a mile away, the boiler exploded with a roar and the smokestack shot in the air like an arrow. The pilothouse followed, with the captain still inside shouting orders.

The explosion lit up the day and blew a hole in the bottom of the ship. Passengers were pitched over the side as if shot from slingshots. Praiseworthy and Jack were among them.

The next thing Jack knew he was underwater and the gold pouches, heavy as lead, were pulling him down. He fought to come up, but the weights kept dragging him below. Then, fighting for his life, he unbuckled his belt. Buckskin pouches and four-shooter fell away into the deep. Seconds later he bobbed to the surface. He spit water and looked around. The riverboat was gone. So was Praiseworthy.

But a moment later his partner appeared, breaking

surface about ten feet away. Jack felt a quick throb of relief. He wiped the wet hair out of his eyes.

"Hang on, partner," said Praiseworthy, shoving over a splintered plank of wood. "Are you all right?"

"Ruination!" cried Jack. "I—I unbuckled my belt!"

Praiseworthy's whiskers were running with sea water. "Think nothing of it, Jack. I had to do the same thing!"

Within ten minutes there were several boats alongside fishing passengers out of the bay. When Praiseworthy and Jack landed at the Long Wharf they were not only as penniless as the day they had arrived, but soaking wet to boot. They had struck it rich, but their fortune was somewhere in the deep of the bay.

"Gone forever," Jack muttered softly.

But Praiseworthy was undaunted. "Mere bits of colored metal," he grinned. "We have our good health, damp as it may be at the moment. The captain gave us a very expensive bath, you might say."

They wouldn't be returning to Boston with their pockets full of gold nuggets, but return they must. Aunt Arabella would need them even more now with everything at home sure to be lost.

They had hardly climbed up the boatstairs to the

wharf when Jack noticed the *Lady Wilma* still riding at anchor.

"Strange," said Praiseworthy. "Captain Swain had planned to sail home as soon as he could unload."

"Maybe he'll let us work our passage back," said Jack.

"A first-rate idea," remarked Praiseworthy.

Without delaying even to dry out they borrowed a skiff and rowed to the *Lady Wilma*. Once alongside they shipped their oars and Praiseworthy raised his hands to his mouth.

"*Hellooo*," he called.

There came no answer. There wasn't even a sound from the other ships at anchor nearby. It was as if they had rowed into a graveyard of sailing vessels.

Finally they climbed aboard, and looked around.

"The crew's gone," said Praiseworthy. "There's not a soul on deck."

"It's spooky," said Jack.

Praiseworthy shouted up at the pilothouse. "Captain Swain!"

There was no reply, except from a cat sunning himself on a rotting mound of canvas. Soon another cat appeared from the fo'c'sle hatch and when Jack looked up he saw a cat walking along one of the yardarms.

"There's nothing here but cats," Jack said. "Those cats from Peru."

"And they appear to have multiplied," Praiseworthy nodded.

They went searching through the ship and everywhere they looked were Peruvian cats and kittens. When they peered into the hold they saw the cargo still there, waiting to be unloaded. Rats had gnawed into barrels of smoked fish and the cats had fattened themselves on rats and fish.

"What has happened here?" Praiseworthy mused. "It looks like Captain Swain has simply abandoned his ship." He scratched through his whiskers. "Left it to all these cats."

A yellow kitten was winding itself around Jack's legs and he picked it up. This morning they had pockets full of gold dust and nuggets. Now they couldn't pay their fare home. He wondered how they would ever get back to Aunt Arabella and Constance and Sarah.

"Strange," said Praiseworthy again.

They returned to the skiff and Jack put the kitten in his shirt. They tied up at the Long Wharf and walked into town and tried to find Captain Swain. Instead, they found Mr. Azariah Jones, the Yankee trader.

He was standing outside an auction tent beside a barrel of free pickles. "Confound it!" he said with a hearty laugh. "I recognize the boy—but is that you behind the whiskers and the red miner's shirt?"

"It's me," said Praiseworthy.

"Help yourself to the pickles. I've become an auctioneer. You have bad luck in the diggings?"

"You might say so," said Praiseworthy.

"Help yourself to the pickles. You look hungry."

"Thank you sir," said Jack. "I am."

"What happened to Captain Swain and the *Lady Wilma?*" asked Praiseworthy.

"The same thing that happens to almost every other ship that comes in here with the gold fever. His crew ran off to the diggings. Why, there are more than two hundred ships out there, rotting at anchor. Deserted. Captain Swain couldn't even hire enough men to unload his cargo. Finally, he just gave up in disgust and got himself a passage home. Have a pickle."

"Is Dr. Buckbee still in San Francisco?" asked Praiseworthy. He tried a pickle.

"Not him. He got over the fever and gave up on that gold map of his. I heard he was horse doctoring somewhere up the river. Doing fine, too. Me, I'd be doing fine if the rats don't put me out of the Cheap John business. Town's full of 'em. Why, a man can hardly stand still at night without something beginning to gnaw on his feet. Blame it, I just got hold of some flour from Chile and the rats are stealing me blind."

"Rats?" said Praiseworthy.

"Did you say rats?" remarked Jack.

Mr. Azariah Jones nodded. "I auctioned off a cat yesterday for fifteen dollars."

"Cats?" said Praiseworthy.

"Did you say cats?" remarked Jack, pulling the kitten from his shirt.

Mr. Azariah Jones clutched the kitten as if it were a nugget of gold.

Praiseworthy gave Jack a wink and looked Mr. Azariah Jones squarely in the eye. "Why, I can safely say that Jack and I can supply you with an unlimited supply of ratting cats. Just provide us with a couple of bags and we'll be back."

The cat auction drew such a crowd that the street was almost blocked. Every storekeeper needed a ratter and the bidding was spirited. Midway through the auction the signal on Telegraph Hill announced the arrival of a sailing vessel, but hardly a soul left the auction. By late afternoon Praiseworthy and Jack had a clink of gold pieces in their pockets. Their share of the cat money ran to almost four hundred dollars.

They wandered toward the Long Wharf to see about passage home. The sailing vessel had dropped anchor and now passengers were coming ashore. Suddenly Jack stopped. He saw a young girl in a dark traveling dress that reminded him of his sister Sarah. Beside her was a taller girl who reminded him of his sister Constance. Beside *them* was a woman in a straw hat and green eyes who looked *exactly* like Aunt Arabella.

It *was* Aunt Arabella!

Jack could barely believe his eyes. And then he realized that even Praiseworthy had stopped in his tracks.

But the woman and two young girls passed them by as if they were total strangers.

"Sarah!" Jack cried out.

The smallest girl turned.

"Constance!" Jack exclaimed.

The other girl turned.

"Miss Arabella!" said Praiseworthy.

The woman turned. And then, suddenly, despite the disguise of jackboots, the rough red miners' shirts and the slouch hats, she recognized her nephew and the butler who had left Boston so many months before.

"Jack! Jack, dear!" cried Aunt Arabella.

There was a shout of joy and they rushed back toward each other. Jack was engulfed in arms.

Praiseworthy stood at a slight distance behind. And then, wiping an eye with her handkerchief, Aunt Arabella straightened and smiled and said, "Hello, Praiseworthy."

"Hello, Miss Arabella."

"You're so changed. Both of you!"

"Yes, miss."

"I'm delighted to see you, Praiseworthy."

"I'm astonished to see you, Miss Arabella—and Miss Constance and Miss Sarah."

Suddenly they were all talking at once.

"We sold the old house," said Constance.

"Soon as we could," said Sarah.

"It was so big and so full of musty old memories," Aunt Arabella said, smiling now. "When we discovered Jack's note on the tea service—that the two of you were running away to California, the girls and I couldn't wait to follow you. It was time to rid ourselves of that house— of the past. It's like being free of a curse. Let me look at you!"

"Did you find gold?" Sarah blurted out.

"Plenty of it," Jack said proudly. "And I drink coffee now."

"Coffee!" exclaimed Constance.

"They call me Jamoka Jack in the diggings."

"How dreadful," Aunt Arabella laughed. She turned back to Praiseworthy, regarding him with a green-eyed twinkle. "And what do they call you?"

"Bullwhip, miss."

"How fearful. What has happened to your black hat and coat and umbrella?"

"Gone. If clothes make the man, as they say, Miss Arabella—I suppose I'm a miner now. Perhaps it's time I shed the past myself."

"You make a very striking miner, it seems to me," Aunt Arabella smiled.

"Out here, one man is as good as another."

"Only more so," said Jack.

Aunt Arabella stood very straight. "I've always believed it."

"Will you be returning to Boston?" asked Praiseworthy.

"Certainly not."

That changed everything and Praiseworthy crimped an eye, just like Pitch-pine Billy. Then he scratched through his whiskers. "In that case—" He stopped to gather up his courage. "I mean—"

"Yes?" said Aunt Arabella.

"If I'm no longer a butler—what I'm trying to say is—well, in California we say a thing straight out."

Aunt Arabella smiled. "Then do stop beating around the bush, Praiseworthy."

"You see—"

"Yes?"

"I mean, women are scarce out here, Miss Arabella. Before you can walk a block you're going to have ten proposals of marriage."

"How delightful."

"What I mean to say is—"

"Yes?"

He cleared his throat. "Maybe this isn't the time or the place, Miss Arabella, but when a man strikes gold he doesn't lose any time staking a claim." With sudden decision, Praiseworthy whipped off his hat. His mouth was as dry as a cured salmon, but he kept talking. "If there's going to be any proposals of marriage I intend to be the first in line. I've got no vices to speak of, although I have taken to smoking strong cigars. To say it right out, Miss Arabella, will you do me the honor of becoming my wife?"

Constance and Sarah began jumping up and down on their toes. "Oh, do, Aunt Arabella! We know you gave him your picture—a long time ago."

"He carries it in his shirt pocket!" Jack exclaimed.

Aunt Arabella was smiling through a wet sparkle in her eyes. "Marry you? Why, of course. I thought you'd never ask."

"By the Great Horn Spoon!" Praiseworthy gasped. Jack had never seen him so flustered. He stared. Constance stared. Sarah stared.

Suddenly Praiseworthy gave the three of them a grin. "Youngsters, if you don't stop staring I'll take a hairbrush to you."

Jack was delighted to hear it. He went on gaping and so did Constance and so did Sarah.

Aunt Arabella held her straw hat against a gust of wind. "Then we'll be going back to the gold fields with you, won't we?"

"Oh, it's no place for women and children," said Praiseworthy.

"We'll *make* it a place for women and children."

"We could build a cabin," said Jack. "Like Quartz Jackson."

"Perhaps we could at that," Praiseworthy said. On some hill within sound of the river, he thought. Why, he might even bring along a law book. He could read it at night. The diggings could use some book law and a man had to think of making a future.

Praiseworthy put Aunt Arabella's hand in the crook of his arm and they started walking up the Long Wharf. They looked very much like a family. They felt like a family. They were a family.

THE END

Like this book? You'll love:

Little Women by Louisa May Alcott

Mr. Popper's Penguins by Richard and Florence Atwater

The Enormous Egg by Oliver Butterworth

The Wonderful Flight to the Mushroom Planet
by Eleanor Cameron

Incident at Hawks' Hill by Allan W. Eckert

The Dark Frigate by Charles Boardman Hawes

Goodbye, Mr. Chips by James Hilton

Ben and Me by Robert Lawson

Mr. Revere and I by Robert Lawson

Maniac Magee by Jerry Spinelli